MEN OF INKED, BOOK SIX

HONOR ME

www.chellebliss.com

CHELLE BLISS

USA TODAY BESTSELLING AUTHOR

COPYRIGHT

Publisher © Chelle Bliss May 10th 2016
Edited by Lisa A. Hollett
Proofread by F. Wilson, R. Sharon, and M. Follis
Cover Design © Chelle Bliss
Formatted by Chelle Bliss

MEN OF INKED SERIES

Book 1 - Throttle Me
Book 2 - Hook Me
Book 3 - Resist Me
Book 4 - Uncover Me
Book 5 - Without Me
Book 6 - Honor Me
Book 7 - Worship Me

To learn more, please visit ***menofinked.com***

CHAPTER 1
CURSE

JOE

GOD CLEARLY HAD a sense of humor.

First, he dropped an innocent blond bombshell into my lap, which changed my life forever. Never in a million years would I have guessed I'd fall head over heels in love with someone so innocent, but it happened.

I corrupted her thoroughly.

Quickly, too.

I made her mine and never looked back. There wasn't a day that passed that I didn't take stock of my life. I was the luckiest son of a bitch in the world.

Next thing I knew, we had a baby, Gigi. She wasn't just a kid, but one who had me wrapped around her little finger.

She said, "Jump."

My response, "How high, baby girl?"

Gigi rocked my world.

Seriously turned everything upside down.

The moment she was born, nothing else mattered. I never knew that type of love existed until she came screaming into my life. It altered the way I looked at everything, making me more protective of my family than ever before.

When she was just a tiny bundle, I'd sit up with her at night and rock her, telling her my hopes and dreams for her entire life. I had big plans too—the kid was going to be president someday. Actually, she could be anything she wanted. I'd make sure of it.

I spoiled her, too much probably, and it turned her into a tiny monster. She was now my cross to bear, my demon child. The first time she said "Daddy," I knew I was a goner—completely and utterly in love.

Don't get me wrong, Suzy was the love of my life...my soul mate.

She was the one person who truly got me and understood who I was on the inside without judging me for my past indiscretions. She was the mother of my children and would always be the one who did it for me.

When Suzy told me she was pregnant again, I was over the moon happy. I mean, more kids meant more love, right?

But if I was being honest, it terrified me too. Especially when the doctor dropped the news that we were having twins.

Twins.

Double the feedings and even less sleep; nothing would ever be the same again. But like with any kid, whether having one or six, they had a way of creating chaos and havoc out of any situation.

Family had always been my number one priority. It was the thing that kept me moving and helped me stay out of trouble most of my life.

I'd been known to have a temper. I couldn't help that shit. If someone was dumb enough to talk shit, they'd better be willing to put up their fists and back their words up with some strength.

Understand this—I was a good guy.

I'd bend over backward to help a friend.

But cross me, and I'd fuck you up. Hurt someone I love, and I'd put you in the ground.

It was that simple. I was like most red-blooded American men.

Years ago, if you'd told me I'd live in a house filled with women and pink shit everywhere, I would've laughed in your face. But it was my lot in life. Pink had replaced the white space, filling up every corner of my world.

But the journey to get to the place of peace hadn't been an easy one. My road to happiness wasn't paved in gold. It was more like a cobblestone walkway, filled with dips and ridges.

CHAPTER 2
6 MONTHS AGO
SUZY

I WADDLED TO THE CHAIR, feeling with my fingertips for the seat before slowly lowering myself. "I can't wait for this to be over," I complained and laid my palms against my round belly.

"Any day now, you're gonna pop," Angel said and laughed.

"Pop isn't really the word that puts a smile on my face, but I feel like that's exactly what's going to happen." My index finger pressed on my belly button. "I feel like a turkey. Ping, I'm ready." If I grew any bigger, I worried my stomach would explode. Bearing mutliples was like being possessed by two demons, and my body wasn't happy about it.

Angel laughed and placed her hands on the sides of my stomach. "I wish I could have another." The lines on her forehead grew more severe as her hands moved around my girth.

"You can have another," I told her, my heart squeezing at the sadness on her face.

"No," she sighed. "I asked Thomas to get fixed. We're done."

Wow. I gawked at her, along with everyone else at the table. "What? You did? Why?"

She shrugged and pulled her hands away. "One is enough for me. He's older, and we're both so busy with work, it just felt right."

"It seems like you regret it, Angel," Mia said, placing her hand on Angel's arm. "It can be reversed."

She shook her hand and swallowed. "I'm fine with the decision. Sometimes, when I see your bellies, I'm a bit envious. But then I remember the feedings, sleepless nights, and potty training, and I get over it really quick." She smiled and grabbed the bottle of vodka sitting in the middle of the table.

"When did he have the surgery? He never mentioned anything," Max said, staring at Angel over the rim of her glass as she took a sip of her vodka and cranberry.

"A few months ago. The best part about it is that we can fuck like monkeys and never have to worry about me getting knocked up."

"I may have to bring up a vasectomy to Joe. I can't imagine going through this again. This is a two-for-one deal." After the girls were born, I was officially closing this chapter in my life. These would be the last two I'd ever carry, and I was happy about that.

"Me too." Izzy clapped her hands. "My shit is closed for business." Izzy nodded definitively. "James may freak, but if he wants to 'fuck like a monkey,'" she said, doing air quotes, "then he better get fixed."

"It sounds like we're talking about dogs." Mia laughed and slapped the table. "Speaking of them, what are they doing in the garage?"

"Working on the old clunker Joe bought." I wrapped my hands around the bottle of water, wishing for once in my life I could actually drink.

"They're probably drinking beer and bullshitin' just like us." Izzy rolled her eyes. "They don't fool anyone."

"It gives us girl time, so I don't care," I said, watching Izzy as she fidgeted with the collar around her neck. "Why aren't you guys at the club tonight? I thought you always went on Friday nights."

"We're going tomorrow night instead. They're having some special demonstrations." Izzy grinned and tugged on her collar.

"Demonstrations?" Max swallowed hard and leaned across the table. "Do tell."

"Throughout the month, different Masters have classes to teach other Masters and subs about new techniques or how to stay safe."

"So what are they teaching about tomorrow?"

Max asked and slid her finger across her bottom lip. "Sounds hot."

Izzy giggled softly. "There are two tomorrow. First is about shibari."

"What's that?" Max interrupted. "Sounds dangerous."

"It's not dangerous. It's about rope play."

Max's mouth fell open and I couldn't help but laugh. "What are you laughing at? Did you know what it was?"

Everyone thinks I'm innocent, but I'm not. I nodded with a giant smile. "I read a lot. I knew what it is, and it sounds sexy."

"Ain't no one tying my ass up with a rope." She shook her head and waved her hands. "Never happening."

"What's the other demonstration about?" Angel asked, resting her head in her palm.

"ElectroSex, specifically violet wands."

Mia spits out her drink, spraying it across the table. "What the fuck?" Mia's head jerked back.

"Oh, that sounds amazing," I said, cradling my belly in my arms.

Max covered her face and peered at Izzy through her fingers. "What the hell is a violet wand?"

Izzy fumbled with her collar and bit her lip. "Um, think of it like a wand that looks like a neon light but shoots out tiny electrical currents. Does that make sense?"

Max gasped. "You let him electrocute you?"

I looked down at the floor, unable to look Max in the eyes because her expression was priceless.

"He's not electrocuting me. It's just another form of play. The tiny sparks are amazing."

"Fuck that shit," Max mumbled and dragged her hands down her face. "You girls got some weird ideas about fun. Ropes, electricity, collars. I just don't understand. What's wrong with good old-fashioned cock?"

"Ain't nothing wrong with cock, Max," Izzy laughed and rubbed her hands together. "Sometimes it's nice to try out new things. What's your favorite toy?"

Max almost went cross-eyed. "I'm not telling you about my toys."

"You're a prude," Angel teased. "I bet you have a giant dildo at home."

"Stop!" Max held up her hand and shushed Angel. "Anthony has a giant cock, why do I need bigger?"

"Nipple clamps?" Izzy raised an eyebrow.

Max glanced at her watch and cleared her throat. "Well, look at the time. I better get home so the babysitter can leave." She started to stand, and Mia put her hand over Max's.

"Sit your ass down," Mia told her, not letting her walk away.

Angel pointed toward the chair. "We all know

your husband. He's a kinky bastard like the rest. Don't act like you don't have a giant chest of toys hiding in your house."

"I'm not saying a thing."

"You should all come to the club one night." Izzy tapped her chin and paused. "I'm sure I can schedule a private party."

"Um…" Max mumbled.

"Fuck yeah. I'm in." Angel fist-pumped the air. "I'm game for anything."

"Hello," I said and waved my hands in front of my enormous stomach. "Humans on board."

"We'll wait until you're recovered." Izzy smirked. "Most of the areas are private, but I think I can work something out. It's a good thing James is friends with the owner. This will be perfect." Izzy practically bounced in her chair.

"Pass the vodka," Max said and held out her hand.

"We'll get you liquored up first, Max. Don't worry, you're gonna love it."

I'd often fantasized through the years about clubs just like the one Izzy and James belonged to. I had shared my fantasies with Joe, and he'd sometimes surprise me with a new toy or something kinkier. There wasn't a thing the man did to me that I didn't love.

Although the thought of visiting their club intrigued me, I couldn't imagine waddling in there without sticking out like a sore thumb. Plus, I didn't really think Joe would go for it.

We were in love. Committed to each other forever, but visiting a sex club was something I wasn't sure would be good for our relationship. It could change everything.

CHAPTER 3
HORMONES
JOE

"SUGAR," I whispered in her ear, slowly stroking the inside of her thigh while she slept. Her round belly stuck out of the covers, reminding me that a morning just like this eight months ago probably led us to this situation—knocked up.

The best part of the entire pregnancy?

She was horny all the time.

"Come on, baby." Tenderness laced my voice, but I wanted to be anything but. I had a raging hard-on and couldn't put Gigi on the bus fast enough to slide back into bed.

Suzy had a thing for being woken up with my dick buried deep inside of her. A fantasy she shared with me a long time ago and I took advantage of it, playing it out over and over again at every turn.

Suzy stirred when my fingers traced a path across her pussy. When she didn't wake, my strokes became more demanding and I spread her legs a bit wider with my feet. Her body writhed against the mattress and she rolled onto her side, pushing her ass against my dick.

Grunting softly, I dug my fingers into her hip and cradled her belly in my other hand.

Just as I started to run my hard cock through her wetness—pregnant and horny all the time—my phone rang. "Fuck," I whispered and tucked it under my pillow quickly.

I stilled, waiting for them to leave a voice mail before I could sink myself deep. But before I could, the phone started to ring again.

I jabbed my hand under the pillow, fisting my phone and silencing it with my grip. Rolling off the bed, I headed toward the bathroom so I didn't disturb Suzy and could start right where I left off.

"Hello." I didn't even look before I answered.

"Yo!"

Fucking Mikey. I should've known it was him, but my raging hard-on had clouded my judgment. "What the fuck, man? It's like eight in the morning."

"It's time to get up, princess." He laughed loudly and ignored the fact that I was pissed.

"I am *up*, and you're interrupting some important stuff."

"Oh, shit! Sorry, man."

Peeking through the doorway, I checked on Suzy

before closing it a little more to muffle my voice. "What do you want?" I growled.

"I thought since we're off today we could meet up."

"For what?" My jaw was clenched so hard it started to ache more than my balls.

"Lunch."

"Yeah, man. I'll be there at noon. Not a minute before. Don't call back." I hung up and turned the ringer off so he couldn't disturb us again. Then I tossed my phone on the counter next to the sink.

When I walked back into the bedroom, Suzy was sprawled out on her side, her large belly keeping her from rolling over. *Perfect.* I crawled back in bed, stroking my shaft as I inched closer to her. "Sugar," I whispered into her ear and nudged my dick against her.

"What?" she moaned and started to stir.

I didn't answer with words, but by thrusting my hardened cock into her waiting, greedy pussy. Being inside of her was pure fucking heaven. There wasn't a day that went by that I didn't want to bend her over some piece of furniture and have my way with her. When she was pregnant, she was usually game, when she wasn't too exhausted—which was rarely the case.

Pregnant Suzy was my favorite Suzy.

She pushed back against me as I withdrew slowly and rammed back into her. Nothing got me harder than the noise she made when I was buried balls deep inside of her. "Whose pussy is this?" I asked, fisting her hair in my hand.

Tipping her head back, she peered up at me and looked straight into my eyes. "Yours. Always yours."

The way she stared at me, her pussy clenching around my cock, my dick hardened even more. Impossible to even imagine, but with her half the time, I thought it would break off before I could come.

"Whose dick is that?" she asked, her mouth hanging open slightly.

"Yours," I growled, repeating her words. "Always yours."

The corner of her mouth twitched and she blinked a few times. "Are you sure?"

My body stilled, leaving her impaled. "What does that mean?"

"Nothing." Her voice cracked and she diverted her eyes.

Tugging lightly on her hair, I pulled her head back so I could see into her eyes. "What did that mean, sugar?"

Lately, she'd said some things that I wrote off as hormones, but with me buried deep inside her, I couldn't shake off the feeling that there was something more to it.

"Nothing, baby. Nothing." She smiled, but it wasn't her typical, happy as a pig in shit smile.

This one was completely fake.

I pulled out and rolled us over so that I was on my side, and I cradled her face in my hands. "Sugar, what's on your mind?" I tried to read the pain I could see in her eyes.

"Nothing," she squeaked, her eyes filling with tears.

"One thing we are is always honest. *Please* tell me."

My heart ached as I stared down at her. Suzy and I always had a passionate, lighthearted relationship—until now.

"I'm just gross," she whispered and closed her eyes, letting the tears spill down the side of her face.

Every ounce of air I had inside my lungs evaporated. "Sugar, you're absolutely stunning." How could my beautiful, supersexy wife think that she was gross?

"You're just saying that because you have to. Look at me, Joey. I'm enormous."

"Suzy." My voice was firm because I needed her to understand I was completely serious. "You're just as beautiful as the day I rescued you on the side of the road." She bit her lip and looked away. My thumb brushed against her cheek and I wanted to take away her pain and self-doubt. "I love you, Suzy."

"I just can't." She wiggled out from underneath me and started to struggle to the edge of the bed. Her belly had grown so large with the twins that she couldn't get out without a lot of energy or help.

"Fucking shit!" Her arms flailed, and no matter how hard she tried, she couldn't get to her feet.

I scooted over, about to give her a little help, when she turned to me and snarled, "Don't." I withdrew my hand. The look of a wild animal in her eyes had me backtracking. My sugary sweet baby girl had vanished, and the devil had taken up residence.

After she climbed off the bed in the most ungraceful way, she scurried to the bathroom and slammed the door.

Collapsing on my back, I stared up at the ceiling and exhaled. I wanted to take all of her pain, take the stress of the babies, and take everything away from her that was ripping her apart. The drawers near the sink in the bathroom opened and slammed. The water turned on and I heard her curse.

I scrubbed my hands down my face because as soon as the word *fuck* left her mouth, I knew that something big was simmering under the surface. With the babies coming soon, we needed to settle this shit between us.

I wanted my wife back, and I wouldn't let her push me away for some crazy fantasy she had in her head that wasn't my reality.

CHAPTER 4
FUCK PREGNANCY

SUZY

MY LIFE HAD BEEN TAKEN over by the babies that grew inside of me. They were so large, I couldn't see my feet or do anything without being reminded that I was as big as a freaking house.

Being pregnant with Gigi was easy, and I thought this pregnancy would be the same. Little did I know that my guy would knock me up with twins. His sperm just had to be so strong that it found a way to hook up with two eggs and not the typical one.

He was all perfection.

I gained pounds every week while the little beasts grew inside of me.

Him?

Not an ounce.

He still had his six-pack and bulging biceps. Beautifully handsome with his dark hair and turquoise blue eyes that saw deep into my soul when I looked at him.

Every day when I glanced down at my ever-growing belly, I cursed myself. It's one thing to be pregnant, and it's quite another to let it get out of control. I felt, no matter how hard I tried to keep my weight under control, I just grew bigger.

How could he love me like this? I stared down and tried to remember what it was like to see my feet on the ground. I'd hit Weeble-wobble status and I was sick of it.

I lost it when we were having sex. How could he say those dirty things to me and mean them with how I looked?

There's no way my perfectly built husband thought I was as beautiful as the day we met. I was riddled with stretch marks and a stomach as big as a beach ball.

"Sugar." Joe knocked on the door while I sat on the edge of the tub, feeling sorry for myself.

"Go away." I already regretted the way I acted—storming off like an idiot and opening my big mouth in the first place.

He didn't deserve to be punished because of how I felt about myself. He'd never done anything to make me feel less than loved and adored, but it was too easy for doubt to creep in every time I looked at myself.

"Open the door or I'm knocking it down."

"Are you going to yell at me?" I grimaced and

waited for his reply, which I'm sure was about to go from upset to pissed off in a hurry.

A loud thud sounded and I heard his voice clear as day. "Baby, I'm not going to yell at you. We need to talk." The handle jiggled. "Open the door."

I pushed myself up, more like a contortionist than a woman, and reached for the door. "Oh, fuck," I said before I could unlock the door, doubling over in the most extreme pain.

Fucking hell—contractions.

I hadn't missed them. I would have liked to have said they were the worst part of labor, but when they cut you open to make more room for the baby… Yeah, that was the worst.

I did my Lamaze breathing just as I'd remembered, and like last time, that shit didn't work.

"Suzy!" Joe shouted and turned the handle again. "Are you okay, baby?"

Damn it. Hunched over in so much pain, I waited for it to pass before I could let him in. "My water broke. Gimme a minute." I clutched the sink and breathed through the final moments of my first contraction.

I could hear him breathing heavily, pacing outside the door separating us, and I was *almost* thankful to be in labor.

I no longer had to explain my behavior.

He'd flip out if I did. Joe loved me. He adored me. Cherished me like no man ever had, but being as big as a house and having two humans growing inside of me… I didn't feel good enough.

"Suzy!" He pounded on the door frantically. "Open the door!"

"Coming," I groaned, moving like I was walking on glass because I knew another contraction was soon to follow. I turned the lock, slowly stepping back to lean against the bathroom sink.

He walked in and scooped me into his arms like I weighed nothing. "We've got to get to the hospital."

"Joe!" I squealed, panicked he'd drop me if I moved. "Put me down. You're going to hurt yourself."

He glanced down with his eyebrows downward. He gave me a look like I was crazy as he placed me on the bed. "Wait here." He raced around the room, grabbing the already packed suitcase from the closet. "Do you need anything else?" Standing there naked, his hair a mess, I couldn't help but smile at his nervousness.

"You need clothes, for sure." I pointed at him, quirking an eyebrow as my finger drifted down to his beautiful, pierced cock.

"Right." He ran his hand through his hair, messing it up more, and scanned the room. "Fuck. I shouldn't be such a mess. This isn't our first kid."

"Nope." I giggled when he grabbed whatever he could find and threw it on haphazardly. Everything that had just happened before my labor began was wiped away in an instant.

He stood with his hands on his hips and his shirt half on. "How can you be smiling?"

I looked, letting my eyes travel slowly up his body before settling on his handsome face. "You're so adorable when you're flustered." My fingers curled around the edge of the comforter, and I readied myself for another contraction.

"Baby." Joe kneeled and rested his hands on my belly. "I don't know what's going on inside that pretty head of yours, but I won't forget it. You have me completely thrown off. Hopefully, after these two little soul suckers come out, everything will get back to normal."

"I'm sorry."

He shifted and cradled my face in his hands before kissing my lips. "I can't believe soon we're going to have three little ones."

"I know." I smiled and my eyes filled with tears, but not of joy... Yeah, I was happy, but the fear I had overshadowed it.

What if I couldn't be a good mom to three?

What if I couldn't be a good wife?

My days and nights would be filled with feedings, diaper changing, and caring for the little ones. I couldn't see Joe and me having a ton of time together with them around.

I worried for us.

What if I couldn't be the woman he wanted and needed?

Joe's phone buzzed and broke the awkward silence before he had a chance to question me further. As he spoke to his mom, he kept glancing at me. I was never so happy for another contraction to start as I was when he hung up.

My insides squeezed and I could've sworn the two monsters inside me were trying to claw their way through my abdomen instead of readying themselves for a trip the natural way. "Oh." I blew out a breath, huffing with puffed cheeks. "God." I sucked in quickly. *In. Out. In. Out.* My knuckles turned white as I gripped the edge of the bed and held on for dear life.

"Let's go, Sunshine."

"Gigi."

Out. In. Out. In. Hell, these were so much worse than last time.

"Mom will get her from school later. I'm not taking any chances with you. Up." He started to put his arm under my legs when I pushed him away.

"No." I shook my head and felt my muscles start to relax. "I'll walk. I'm not having you fall down the stairs with me in your arms." I held my hands out to him, looking for a little help.

He grabbed my hands before he straightened and pulled me with him. "You never worried I'd drop you before." He wrapped an arm around my waist like I needed his support to move.

"I've never been this big before." I placed my hand on my stomach and tried to remember what it was like to see my feet when I walked, but I drew a blank.

"Stop talking like that. You're stunning and carrying my babies inside you."

I glanced down at the floor to avoid his eyes. "Fine," I mumbled. "I'm fat, but whatever."

"Sugar, when you're healed, I think you need a spanking."

My eyes flickered to his and my cheeks instantly heated. The look in his eyes was one I'd seen before. There'd be hell to pay, and his torture implement would be his cock. "Yes, sir." I couldn't hold back my sarcasm.

With his hand on the small of my back, he led me out of the bedroom and took each step with me. He was ready to catch me if I tumbled forward. When we made it to the bottom of the stairs, another contraction hit me.

"Fuck!" I yelled, doubling over and grabbing his hand, squeezing it with all my might. "They shouldn't be this close together." I glanced up at him, fear coursing through my veins that maybe something was wrong.

I spent hours in labor with Gigi and I remembered having a lot of time between each contraction, but this was different.

The look on his face was absolute panic. My big, strong husband was filled with fear and it freaked me out.

CHAPTER 5
DOUBLE TROUBLE

JOE

WHEN HER CONTRACTIONS came fast and furious, I won't lie, she scared the fuck out of me. Besides Gigi, Suzy was my *everything*.

She was the reason I woke up in the morning. The reason I didn't go to jail for beating the fuck out of some pissant jagoff every day.

I'd be nothing without her. Without her, I didn't work.

"Everything is fine, Mrs. Gallo," The obstetrician reassured us with half her arm up my wife. "You've just dilated quickly. The babies are about ready to come out."

Suzy's mouth was hanging open, so I figured I'd ask what she was thinking. "Already?"

"Sometimes labor is quicker the second time around." She smiled, patting Suzy's leg after withdrawing her arm and snapping off the biggest pair of latex gloves I'd ever seen.

I watched in complete horror and tried not to gag. "Isn't it too early for her to give birth, Doc? She's not full term yet." I stroked Suzy's hair, trying to keep my cool.

"It's perfectly normal with multiples, plus the babies are developed enough at this point to be healthy. Don't worry, Mr. Gallo. I know what I'm doing." She winked, laughing as she tossed the gloves in the trash. "I'll be back in a few minutes and we can start pushing."

When she walked out of the room, Suzy glared at me. "What's this *we* shit? I'm the one with two aliens inside of me, trying to claw their way out of my body. I'm the only one pushing them out of my *tiny* vagina. Not you. Not her. *Me!*" She waved her hands frantically in the air. "I'm the one doing everything while you sit there calm, sexy, and without your body splitting in two. I'm going to be the one tearing wide open as I push two humans and their *giant* Gallo heads out of my body." She collapsed, gasping for air, and closed her eyes.

I bit my lip. Pregnant Suzy was unpredictable, but in-labor Suzy was just downright scary. "I know, sugar. You're doing all the hard work. I'm just here to cheer you on and support you."

Her nostrils flared and her eyes grew wide when she glanced up. "Support me? If you want to support me, you'll never knock me up again. You want to cheer me on?" She rolled her eyes and made a noise low in her throat. "Stop fucking talking."

I braced myself, waiting for her head to do a 360. I brought my mouth right next to her ear. "My sweet little wife, you beg for my cock every day. It takes two to tango, sweetheart. I didn't put you in that bed." I lowered my voice further, whispering, "Your sweet little cunt did."

She closed her eyes again and moaned. "You're just too damn good. I can't keep my hands to myself. It's still your fault, my dear husband."

I couldn't hold it in any longer. I burst into laughter. "Now, I fuck you too good?"

"Yes!" she screeched, pounding her fist on the crappy, plastic hospital bed. "If you weren't so good at it, I wouldn't be lying here right now."

Just as I was about to reply, the nurse walked in. "I hear someone is ready to push." Her voice was so chipper, kind of like my wife's used to sound like before pregnancy. "Are we excited?" she asked, moving a tray of instruments next to the foot of the bed.

"I just want this over. I'm so freaking uncomfortable."

"That makes two of us," I muttered and nodded at the nurse with a fake smile on my face before leaning over and kissing Suzy's forehead. "Ready, sugar?"

She didn't reply. The look she gave me was one I'd seen before. She was cursing me inside, but she was keeping it to herself since we were in mixed company.

"We're as ready as we'll ever be, ma'am," I said.

The nurse blushed, turning the brightest pink I'd ever seen while she pulled the stirrups out for Suzy. "Ma'am, we're just about ready. Let me go get the doctor and we can get started."

"See? Even the sixty-year-old nurse wants you," Suzy said after the nurse walked out.

Pulling her hand to my mouth, I kissed it gently. "Sugar, the only woman I ever want is lying in this bed. Now, instead of giving me attitude, why don't you get a little excited about our babies? Yeah?"

I knew as soon as the words left my mouth that it was the wrong thing to say. I had been through this before. Seen what happened when a woman gave birth. It was the most frightening, godforsaken thing I'd ever experienced. If men gave birth, humans would've been extinct a long time ago. There was no way in hell I'd let that happen to my body. There's no sex in the world worth being split in two. I knew I was being a tad dramatic, but I saw that shit.

"Are you fucking serious right now? Get excited? Fuck you, Joey Gallo," she snarled, and I swore her face morphed into something straight out of a horror movie.

"Did you figure out a name, baby?" I changed the subject quickly.

She placed her hands on her belly, like I'd seen her do a thousand times and stroked it with her thumbs. "I don't care if we call them A and B. I just want them out!"

I pulled her hand from her stomach, rubbing the tender flesh between my fingers. "I think we should name them Luna and Rose."

She rolled her eyes, turning toward the window and away from me. "Whatever is fine."

"Suzy." I squeezed her hand gently. "Look at me." She turned toward me, slowly dragging her eyes to mine as I waited. "I don't know what's happening here, but you need to remember a few things, love."

"What?" Her voice was laced with attitude.

"First of all, I love you more than life itself." I leaned forward and kissed her cheek. "Second, you're still as beautiful as the day I met you. Remember that day, sugar?"

The corners of her mouth turned up, and I could almost see her replaying the moment in her head when I found her on the side of the road. "Yeah." She blinked slowly before sighing.

"When I look at you, I'll always see that scared, beautiful creature in my headlights as I blew by. I knew the moment I saw you that I had to have you. Never forget that you're mine and always will be. I don't care about anything but that."

"But, Joe—"

I put my finger against her lips. "No buts."

She glanced down and swallowed before bringing her eyes back to mine. "I love you. I'm sorry." She sighed. "Will you forgive me?"

I kissed her roughly on the mouth. "There's nothing to forgive, li'l mama."

She grinned, her eyes sparkling at the mention of the nickname before her face changed and her eyes widened. "Oh, God! I have to push."

"Here we are." The doctor looked calm, dressed in full battle gear when she entered. "Are we ready?"

I didn't give Suzy any time to snap back. "Yes."

She sat at the end of the bed and grabbed a new pair of gloves. "How are you feeling, Mrs. Gallo?"

My stomach instantly turned at the memory of Gigi's birth, and I had to do it twice this time.

"I'm good and ready." Suzy placed her feet in the stirrups, peering up at me with scared eyes as I helped her shimmy down the bed to get into position.

I smiled and smoothed away the tiny wisps of hair that had settled near her eyes. "You got this," I said, but I wasn't sure if I did.

Two hours later, lots of screaming, tons of blood, and a whole lot of tears had been shed. But I now had three beautiful daughters, along with an amazing wife.

I snuggled Rosie close, kissing the top of her head.

"Hey, sweet girl." I peered into her dark eyes, still glazed over from the trauma of birth. She let out a tiny noise and squirmed in my arms, and I gripped her tighter. "I've waited so long to meet you, Ro. Now that you're here, I'm never going to let you go." I rested my lips against her tiny little cheek, feeling the softness of the newborn skin as the enormity of the moment finally crashed over me. Turning my body to face Suzy, I watched as she held Luna in her arms, whispering sweet nothings in her ear much the same way I was with Ro.

The only one missing from the room was Gigi. She had been so excited to become a big sister. She'd squealed with delight when we talked about all the things she could teach them. And she was thrilled she'd finally have some play friends, even though it would take a couple of years.

I settled next to Suzy, resting my arm with Ro on the bed, and smiled as I looked at my family. Suzy had gone through delivery like a trooper. A batshit crazy one, but still, she did it. "Hey," I whispered.

"Hey," she whispered back with a smile.

"It's all done. Now comes the hard part."

"Says the man with his nether regions still intact." She scoffed.

I chuckled, trying not to jostle the baby. "This is the last moment of silence we'll probably have for a very long time."

"I know." She frowned, pushing the edge of the

blanket away from Lu's face. "I don't know if I'm ready, Joe." Her face was riddled with fear and apprehension.

"I'll be there every step of the way, sugar. My mom will stay over as long as you need her too. You're not alone in this."

"We need to talk," she said, and my stomach plummeted.

"Hey," Ma said when she popped her head in the door, drawing our attention away from each other.

"Come in." Suzy motioned to my mother and pretended like she hadn't just said the words that instantly make every sane person's stomach drop.

We need to talk.

"Oh my God, they're so tiny," Ma said, approaching the bed with Pops right behind her. "Look, Sal, more girls to spoil."

"Hi, Suzydoll. How are you, love?" Pop asked, leaning over the bed and kissing her gently on the head.

"I've been better." Suzy gave him a sweet smile. "Want to hold Lu? Wait. Is this Ro? I'm so confused."

Ma elbowed him when he started to reach for the baby. "Not before me. Don't worry, Suzy, twins can be challenging but you'll be fine."

"Mar, there are *two* babies," Pop reminded her, rubbing the spot she just bruised.

"Here, Pop, hold Rosie for me. My arms are getting tired." I lied, but I knew my parents were just as excited as we were for the new arrivals. We'd have them all to ourselves soon enough.

"Where's Gigi?" Suzy settled back into the bed after Ma took Lu from her arms.

"She's out with Izzy. They're playing 'I Spy' to keep her mind occupied until she can come in."

I grabbed my wife's hand and gave it a quick squeeze. "I better go out and let her know Suzy is okay. Want me to bring her back with me, sugar?"

"Yeah. I need to see her." She smiled halfheartedly. I knew there was so much left unsaid, but I had no idea what she wanted to share. Either way, I had a sinking feeling when I walked out of the hospital room.

I watched for a few moments from around the corner as Gigi jumped up and down and Izzy laughed. They were spitting images of each other. She may have been mine, but she was a mini Izzy in the making and it scared the crap out of me.

"Daddy," she said, catching my eye before running toward me and jumping into my arms.

Wrapping my arms around her, I gave her the biggest hug and twirled around in a circle. "Hey, baby girl. Are you having fun with Aunt Izzy?"

Gigi placed her tiny hands on my cheeks, and with the straightest face, said, "She cheats, Daddy."

I laughed, glancing over at Izzy. "She's always been that way, Gig. She has to win at everything."

"It's not fair. I'm widdle. She should let me win."

Her tiny, wet lips connected with mine when she snaked her arms around my neck. "Tell her, Daddy," she whispered and pointed at Izzy, who was now talking to Mike and ignoring us.

"That's not how it works, baby. People just can't let you win." I held back my laughter at the innocent look she gave me, pleading for my help.

"But Mommy lets you win."

My eyebrows rose. "She does?"

She climbed to my side like a little monkey and adjusted her body to curl into her favorite spot in the crook of my arm. "I heard her. She says 'I give in. It's yours. Take it.' and usually makes weird noises, but she always lets you win."

Embarrassment flooded me. "Oh, baby. Mommy is a very sweet woman. Your aunt Izzy isn't so giving."

"I know." She pouted, running her fingers through the back of my hair. "Like when you're playing a game and you tell Mommy, 'I own you.' Mommy knows that she can't win with you, so she just gives it to you."

Oh my God. Clearly Gigi had been hearing us at night. I thought the walls were thicker. The only thing I'm thankful for is that she thinks we're playing *games*, and innocent ones at that.

"Mommy and I are different, sweetie. Want to see your baby sisters?" I changed the subject because, right now, I couldn't even begin to process the possible harm our evenings would cause to my daughter in the future.

She bounced in my arms with the biggest smile. "Yes! Is Mommy okay?"

I rested my lips against her temple as I headed back toward Suzy's room. I inhaled the familiar scent I'd grown to love, the strawberry shampoo Suzy also used on herself. "She's perfect, Gigi. Now you can't talk real loud or you'll scare your sisters."

She placed her finger against her lips. "I'll be really, really quiet, Daddy. Promise."

As soon as I opened the door, Gigi wiggled from my arms and ran toward Suzy, yelling, "Mommy! Mommy!"

That was my Gigi. Nothing would ever be the same again. Quiet time was over and chaos was about to begin.

CHAPTER 6
AVOIDANCE
SUZY

IT HAD BEEN a week since the babies were born. Seven days since I uttered the words, "We need to talk."

I regretted it as soon as they slipped from my lips. Joe hadn't pushed the issue and brought it up. I don't even know what I was going to say. It just came out. I'd like to blame it on the hormones or maybe the stress of the labor, but I was so overcome with emotions that I wanted to get some things off my chest.

"Suzy," Joe whispered next to me.

Lying in the dark, I stared at the ceiling and felt my insides knot. "Yeah?"

He snaked his arm around my middle, resting it against my still soft, pudgy, baby fat. Soft to his hard. "What did you want to say to me after our girls were born? There's something going on, and I need to know. I can't sleep at night. I can barely eat. All I think about is that my wife doesn't love me anymore."

Guilt overcame me and tears began to spill down my face. "I don't know, Joe. I love you. More than anything, I love you." The words stopped as the tears came faster…harder.

"Sugar," he whispered, pulling me closer to his body and resting his lips against my forehead. "What's bothering you? What don't you know?"

My eyes stayed pinned to the ceiling. I couldn't look him in the eye. "How do you love me?"

"How?"

"Yeah." My voice was a whisper as I choked down a sob.

"I don't even understand what that's supposed to mean." He scooted backward, taking me with him as he rested against the tall, wooden headboard. With a few moves, he had me straddling him with my face in his hands, unable to look away. "Tell me what's going on, Suzy."

My heart ached from the look in his eyes. I knew it. Had seen it before. It was complete terror and fear that I had caused by my careless words. "I just don't understand why you want me."

His eyebrows drew together, causing severe creases on his forehead when the power of my words hit him. "You're my wife. I'll always want you."

"That's not true," I replied before he could say

another word. "There are plenty of men who leave their wives."

His head jerked back, his blue eyes narrowing. "You think I'm going to leave you?" After he spoke, his mouth hung open.

I wiped away the tear that hung on my chin before my lip began to quiver. "Why wouldn't you?" My voice cracked when I started to cry harder.

"Baby, I love you, but this is the last conversation we're going to have about this. I'm going to talk to Mia and find someone for you to talk to, because the very thought of not being with you makes my stomach turn." He took a deep breath, blowing it back out slowly. "There isn't a day that goes by that I don't show you how much I love you. There isn't a second that passes that I don't worship the very ground you walk on, sugar. There's no one on this Earth for me but you. The question is... Do you still love me?"

I didn't even have to think about it. "I do. More than anything, I do. I just keep looking at myself, and then I see you and you're perfect. I just don't get it."

"When I look at you," he said as his hands slid down my body, brushing my extra full breasts along the way, "I see the same girl I fell in love with. I love you more today than I loved you the day we got married. Every day with you is like a gift. The fact that you're doubting that has me scared." His hands rested on my hips and his grip became almost bruising.

"You're just too perfect for me," I whispered, admitting the thing I had been thinking for months.

His forehead came to a rest against mine. "I'm the furthest thing from perfect. You know that. You just gave birth to two babies and your hormones are out of whack. I'm not going anywhere. You're mine, sweetheart. When I married you, I didn't make that decision lightly. The day I said 'I do,' it was for life. Do you still want me, Suzy?"

"I do," I whispered and closed my eyes. I couldn't even imagine a life without him. "More than anything in the world."

"We'll get through this together. I'll do anything to make you feel like the most important thing in my life. Never doubt my love for you."

I didn't doubt his love. It was more his *want* for me that I worried about. "Okay."

He pulled my body forward and I placed my head on his shoulder, burying my face in his neck. "I love you, Sunshine."

"Love you too, Joe."

"Tomorrow we start anew. It's time to get some help. It's time to get our life back on track and settle into the new us. We're no longer a three, we're a five. And if we don't watch it, someone's going to get left behind."

I worried I'd be the one left in the dust.

CHAPTER 7
THE ROAD TO HELL AND BACK

JOE

"DO you have time to talk today?"

"Always for you," Ma replied.

"I'll be there in ten."

"I'll be waiting."

I threw the phone in the passenger seat and headed toward my parents' house. I needed to talk to my ma and figure out what to do about Suzy. I figured there was no better person than a woman who had given birth to five children.

Mia, Mike's wife, spent the day with Suzy. She offered to help out so I could go into work. Before I headed home, I decided to stop and talk with my mother and get her thoughts on our relationship. Ma had never guided me wrong, and I knew she'd say the right thing to make me feel better.

After I sat down at the table, she slid a cup of

coffee in front of me and patted my hand. "What's bothering you, Joe?"

"It's Suzy, Ma. I'm worried about her…about us."

"Be patient with her. She's been through a lot."

My finger moved over the rim of the mug, and I watched a stray coffee ground that floated across the top. "I know. She thinks I can't possibly want her. Her body's changed, but I love it the same. She's the only one for me, and I'm struggling to find a way to convey that message."

"Joseph." She touched my hand that had been resting on the table. "There's nothing you can do to make her feel that way. I've seen you with her. Watched you for years. You love that woman something fierce. She needs to realize it for herself. You need to get her into a good therapist, baby. Postpartum depression is a bitch."

I gave her a halfhearted smile. "It started before the babies arrived."

"You've never been pregnant, Joe. God," she said, rubbing her stomach. "I still remember feeling as big as a house. There wasn't a moment I felt sexy the entire time. Your body becomes distorted and enormous. I know exactly how Suzy feels. I didn't understand how your father could possibly be attracted to me. Just give her time or make an appointment with someone. She'll be okay, it'll just take some time."

"I can't wait, Ma. I can't. Every day, I feel like

she's slipping further and further away. I can't sit by idly and watch it happen. I refuse to do it."

"Why don't you talk to Mia when you get home today? See what she says about Suzy and then go from there. I'm sure she can refer you to someone."

"What's wrong with Suzy?" Pop asked when he walked into the kitchen, still holding a golf club in his hand.

"Oh, just baby stuff, Sal." Ma stood quickly, walking toward my father and wrapping her arms around him. "How did you do today?"

"I beat the piss out of the old guy." He smiled, proud of his accomplishment.

"You really should let him win sometimes."

"Hell no, Mar. No man in his right mind lets another one win just because of his age. If he beats me, it'll be fair and square."

"But he's one of our biggest donors," Ma told him, and she pushed him in the chest, pretending to be mad.

"I always beat him and he still gives the money. Any idea why, dear?"

She scurried over to the coffeepot and poured a cup for him. "Enlighten me."

He sat down across from me and rested the club in the corner near the window. "Every time we play, we wager on his donation. If he wins, I pay his money every year. If I win, he doubles his donation."

My mother turned, cup in hand, and gaped at

my father. "All these years I thought he was generous, but you've just been beating him into submission."

My father's crooked smile and wink made my stomach queasy. "He's not the only one."

"Salvatore!" She shot him the look of death before changing the subject. "By the way, your brother called from Chicago."

My head jerked back slightly. "I thought he was still in prison."

Pop waved his hand. "Nah, the old bastard's out. He's having some trouble with the bar and wanted my advice."

"What's going on with the bar?" I asked.

"You don't want to know," he said and scrubbed his hands down his face. "Santino is his own man and doesn't always live life like the rest of us."

"He sure was a handsome devil, though," Ma added.

"Oh, yeah, Mar?" Pop reached out and rubbed her cheek. "Don't forget who owns you."

Oh, for fuck's sake. I was my father. Yikes. "I'm out. I can't listen anymore, and I'm sure Suzy could use some help."

"You never could handle our love." Pop chuckled and slid his arm around Ma's back as she came to stand next to him.

"There's only so much of it I can take before the bile rises up my throat. You two have fun." I started toward the door, leaving them to whatever they had planned next.

"I plan on it!" Pop yelled just as I turned the handle.

"Gross," I muttered, walking into the sunshine, wishing I could scrub the last few minutes from my mind.

When I walked through the front door, Mia had Rosie in her arms, sitting on the couch. "Where's Suzy?" I asked before tossing my keys on the small table near the door in the foyer.

"Sleeping. She was exhausted." Mia smiled down at the baby and tickled her feet. "I miss the time when they're little." She sighed.

"You can come over any time and babysit, sis."

She laughed and pushed back her straight, brown hair. "I may just take you up on that."

Sitting down next to her, I looked toward the stairs. "Are you sure she's asleep?"

"Completely. She was like a zombie and lay down about thirty minutes ago. I figure she'll be out for at least another hour."

"She's been staying up at night with the babies. I keep trying to get her back to bed and I stay up as long as I can, but damn, she's stubborn."

"That's part of being a mom, Joe."

"I want to talk to you about something, Mia. But this stays between us. Understand?" I glanced down at Rosie just as her eyes closed.

"You know I won't say a word. What's up?"

"It's Suzy. She's been really depressed. I don't know what to do to help her. I wanted to know what you thought after spending the day with her."

She adjusted her body to face me and her hazel eyes bored into me. "Now that you mention it, I was going to talk to you about getting her to talk to someone. Typically, she's so bubbly and happy, but there's something off, which is completely normal for some women after giving birth. But you never want to let things fester."

I rubbed my hands against my jeans. "Do you know of anyone she can talk with?"

"Yeah, I'll give you the number for the woman I saw after Lily was born."

My eyebrows shot up because I never knew Mia had postpartum depression. "You went through it too?"

"It's common, Joe. Happens to the best of us. Hormones are all out of whack in our bodies before the baby is born, and especially after. Having a new little one is exhausting, and it can make us question everything. Just make sure to get her in to speak with Karen as soon as possible."

"Text me the number later and I'll set it up."

"Can do." She leaned forward, holding out Rosie.

"I better run and get home. I'm sure Mike and Lily have destroyed the house."

"That's a given." I laughed. He was a human wrecking ball, and his little girl was just a small version of him.

"Give Suzy my love. Call me whenever you need a reprieve."

"I will," I told her before she gathered her things and left.

Sitting in the living room with Rosie in my arms, I wondered how long it would be before I had my wife back. I missed her bubbly sunshine. The kind where a simple look could have me giddy with excitement.

We'd get there again. I'd wait, even if took a lifetime.

Suzy lay sprawled out on the bed with her robe wrapped tightly around her when I pushed open the door. I didn't speak as I crawled into the bed next to her and pulled her against me. Burying my face in her hair, I let her scent surround me—the strawberries and sweetness that I loved so much.

"I'm so tired," she whispered and curled into me. "So tired."

"Why don't we go to sleep, love?" I brushed the hair off her neck, exposing her skin and resisting the urge to kiss it.

"I don't think I can sleep." She sighed and stared at the wall.

I hoisted myself up on my elbow and pulled backward so I could see her face. My stomach knotted at the distant look in her eyes. "Sugar, I think you need some help."

She dragged her eyes to mine, staring at me for a moment before squeezing them shut. "I think you're right, Joe."

I stroked her cheek, wishing I could take her pain away. "I love you more than life itself. I'll be with you every step of the way, love."

She stared up at me with tears in her eyes. "Thanks, baby. You can't help me out of this, though."

"I know," I said, wiping away the tears as they fell. "I'll make an appointment for you to talk to someone."

She turned to her side, weeping into my shirt. I rocked her, rubbing her back, and said a silent prayer for the love of my life.

CHAPTER 8
LIFE UNFILTERED

SUZY

I SPENT my life being in control.

Every moment planned out.

I had lists for my lists. I wasn't the type of girl who winged anything. I'd never been able to be a free spirit. Joe had changed me slightly, but I still had my OCD tendencies that needed to be fulfilled. When the babies arrived and everything seemed to be out of my control, I sank deep and felt helpless.

It consumed me. Overtaking every bit of my life and overwhelmed me.

By the time I walked into the therapist's office, I was ready to make a change and gain some of my control back...become the master of my own destiny again.

It was the hardest thing I ever had to do—delving into the darkest corners of my psyche. There were things lurking there that I hadn't shared with another soul. Not even my husband or best friend.

It didn't happen right away.

At first, our sessions were about how I felt that day and how things were at home. She never passed judgment, always kept her face devoid of emotion, and just listened. After a while, I felt like sharing more. I'd tell her stories about Joe or our children, and that would lead to a barrage of questions. She didn't bombard me with them, but she'd ask them as if we were having a casual conversation over drinks.

Little by little, I exposed every crack in my carefully constructed veil of happiness. As a mom and a wife, I put on the mask I was expected to have in public. There was always a smile on my face, even when inside I felt nothing. I laughed when it was called for and pretended to be happy.

I even tried to put that happy facade on for Joe. But sometimes, when my guard was down, the mask would slip and I'd be exposed. I couldn't hide it forever. Joe knew me too well for him not to see how I truly felt. He probably knew before I even realized he'd caught on.

"How does that make you feel?" Karen, my therapist, asked after I let it slip that women came on to my husband in front of me in the most blatant and obvious ways.

"Unworthy," I mumbled and stared out the

window, watching the raindrops as they splashed against the sill.

"Why?"

"He's just so beautiful, and many of the women trying to get his attention are too. I know exactly what I look like."

"And how is that?"

"Gross." The frown lingering on my lips deepened.

"Does your husband do anything to make you feel this way? Does he stare at other women and reject you in any fashion?" Even without looking at her, I could tell she was staring at me, appraising me.

"No. He doesn't even notice the women. He's always watching me, flirting with me, and trying to get my attention."

"Then why does it matter what other people do that you can't control?"

"Because I look at them and then I look at me and —" I sighed and glanced down at my hands that were resting in my lap. "I can't see why he stays with me."

She jotted something down in her notebook and my stomach turned. "If Joe were to gain fifty pounds, would you love him less?"

I finally dragged my eyes to hers. "No. He's the love of my life."

She tilted her head, and I could feel her passing judgment. "If he let himself go, would you be any less attracted to him?"

"I'd still want him. Although he's the handsomest man I've ever seen, I'm with him for the way he loves me, not because of his looks."

She chewed on the end of her pen for a moment as we stared at each other. "Why do you think he'd love you any less because of some baby weight you've already started to shed?"

"Because he's just that pretty." I bit my lip and closed my eyes, exhaling the breath I'd been holding. "And he's a man. Men are more visual."

"When we're in love, we're often blind to our partner's supposed flaws. You may think that your body is unattractive, but your husband still looks at you with the same love in his eyes. He sees the woman he fell in love with. Does he ever point out your flaws?"

"Never!" I answered quickly. God, I couldn't love a man who would do that to me. "He claims I don't have any." I laughed softly, probably halfway to the funny farm.

"You wouldn't love him less with flaws or fifty pounds, and he doesn't love you less with baby weight and stretch marks. They're what make you you. They're the storyline of our life. Each mark on our body is a piece of our life story being etched in skin as a remembrance of our journey. Instead of looking at them as a flaw, you should view them as a badge. They're marking an accomplishment or a milestone in our life."

"My sash is just about full, Doc." My eyes drifted to my thigh that had peeked out from my sundress. One of the supposed badges was visible. Whiter than the other skin even though I had lost a lot of the pregnancy weight, the aftermath was still there. Lingering and reminding me of what I used to be.

"Our outsides will always change, Suzy. We can't be young forever. Someday, we'll all grow old and our skin will be riddled with wrinkles and blemishes. We fall in love with the soul of another human being. If you love your husband for the way he loves you, and it seems from our conversations that his love runs deep, then why wouldn't he love you for the same reasons?"

"I don't know." I twisted my hands together and let my eyes drift back to the rainy picture playing out just on the other side of the window.

"This week, I want you to write down any negative comments or situations that occur in which you feel he doesn't love you. Bring the list next week, and we'll see what your triggers are. Maybe if we can determine what brings about the feelings, we can work through them."

That was lingo for: we'll figure out why you're so fucked up. I knew what she was doing. She was trying to prove a point, and for once, after thinking about how much I loved my husband, I decided to play along.

Present Day

It took almost six long months before I felt like myself again. Walking out of Karen's office for the last time, I glanced up at the sky and took in the beauty of it all.

For months, everything looked gray. Like there had been a filter placed over my eyes that made everything dull and lifeless. But now, as I stood there staring up at the big puffy clouds and the bright rays of the sun bouncing off the windows around me, everything and anything seemed possible.

My phone beeped, and I cupped my hand around the screen to block out the light.

> Joe: When is my love coming home? I miss her.

I smiled and felt the warmth of his words stronger than the rays of the sun.

> Me: Give me two hours. I'm meeting the girls for drinks.

> Joe: Call a cab and come home tipsy.

My belly flopped at the idea of a little drunken sex with him. I stopped breastfeeding a month ago, for sanity's sake. I felt like a dairy cow always hooked up to the pumping machine. It was the last step to getting a piece of my soul back.

> **Me:** I'll see what I can do, big boy.

That message earned me a cock photo. His giant hands were wrapped around his even bigger member, with the piercings shimmering in the light.

> **Joe:** We're waiting for you.

I giggled and headed toward the bar three doors down from the doctor's office. When I walked in, Mia, Izzy, Angel, Sophia, and Max greeted me. We were family. All the girls most important to me were here to celebrate the end of my therapy and my return to normalcy.

We did it when Mia finished her therapy after having Lily, and it was only right for me to allow them the same privilege of a girls' night out and a reason to get shit-faced together.

"Here she is!" Izzy announced, holding up her martini in my direction as I walked toward where they were seated.

"I am!" I curtsied, playing up the fact that we were here to celebrate me, even though it was really just an excuse to escape our husbands and kids for the night. "I see you didn't wait for me."

Everyone had a drink in hand, and most of them were half consumed. "We just got here five minutes ago. Don't get your panties in a bunch. Here," Max said, pushing the untouched martini waiting in my spot toward me as I sat.

"It's your favorite." Mia smiled, tipping her glass in my direction.

I licked my lips. The mere thought of the deliciousness in front of me had my mouth watering. When I wrapped my hands around it and brought it toward my mouth, Sophia spoke. "Let's toast, ladies."

Everyone hooted and hollered in excitement. "To Suzy—" Izzy pushed back her chair and raised her glass as she stood. "It's nice to have our girl back. We've missed you. I always wanted sisters, and looking around this table, I realize I have everything I wanted in life. We're a family. We love you, Suzy. Here's to our sisterhood."

"Drink up, ladies. We have a long night ahead of us," Angel added before taking a small sip of her drink.

I eyed her over the rim of my glass, but she diverted her eyes. When the cupcake martini slid across my tongue, there was an explosion of taste I could only describe as orgasmic. The deliciousness of the mind-altering vodka and sweet white chocolate liqueur sliding down my throat had my head spinning.

"Slow down, partner," Mia said, placing her hand on my arm.

I turned to her with the biggest smile on my face. "Just figured I'd catch up."

Mia laughed and shook her head. "We don't need you drunk after only one drink, Suz."

"It takes more than that, Mia. I'm not completely a lightweight drinker anymore."

"That's right, bitches. That's because of me," Izzy added. "No more virgin daiquiris for that girl. She's a big girl now. Has the panties to prove it, too."

I leaned forward with the glass still in my hand but holding it carefully so as not to spill an ounce. "Not today, Iz. I didn't put any on," I confessed and felt dirty and sexy at once.

"I don't want to know," Izzy said, waving her hand in front of me.

"Your brother doesn't like when I wear them anymore."

"Stop!" Izzy placed her hand in front of my face. "Don't say anything more."

Sophia elbowed her and laughed. "Don't listen to her. We all want to know. How is Joe?"

My belly rolled at the mention of my husband. "Sexier than ever, Soph."

"Fuck," she hissed, throwing back her martini like it was water before setting the glass down on the table. "Do all you bitches have pierced junk at home?"

Everyone smirked, knowing that what they had was special and totally freaking amazing.

Sophia dragged her hands down her face and grunted. "I hate you all. Kayden won't get his dick pierced. He said he doesn't need it to give me what I need."

Kayden, her husband, had always been a trip. He never lived life in the shadow of anyone else. Their life hadn't always been easy, but their love was much like that of Joe and myself—meant to be.

"You're not missing out on anything." I tried to make her feel better.

"Lies," she groaned.

"Pierced or not, we're all pretty damn lucky," Max said before waving over the waitress for another round.

"Yeah," I sighed.

"Speaking of dicks, what's the plan tonight?" Mia asked Izzy.

"We're going to see a dick or two." Izzy giggled and took a sip of her martini with a glimmer of mischief in her eyes.

"Ladies," I said, my voice almost a song. "I'm going to have to pass on seeing a penis that isn't my husband's."

"You're such a pussy," Angel chimed in, and it took everything in me not to spit out my drink. She typically didn't use that word, and it took me completely by surprise.

"Yeah, she is. I thought maybe some of my dirty had rubbed off on her, but clearly she needs an 'attitude adjustment,' as James calls it."

I rolled my eyes and ignored their nonsense. I

wasn't a pussy for not wanting to see the junk of strangers. I was happily in love. Hell, I still lusted after my husband. After months of being depressed and uninterested in sex, I was finally back on the Joe train, and I planned to ride that beautiful cock as much as possible. I wanted to get home to my husband, a little tipsy, and see what he had planned for me. There was no way I was going to a strip club with this group of horny biddies.

"I bet you get a lot of those." Max nudged Izzy's arm and cackled.

Izzy's grin widened. "I can't help myself, plus I'd be lying if I said I hated them. I'm always up for a spanking."

"Jesus," Max mumbled and pretended to gag.

Izzy turned quickly, giving her full attention to Max. "Oh, shut your face, Max! You're a dirty whore too." Izzy wagged her finger in front of Max's face. "Don't act like you're a nun. I know Anthony. I know him better than almost anyone in the world. That man is kinky as fuck and all about the spankings."

"Well…I…" Max cleared her throat. "He doesn't give me an attitude adjustment."

"That's because he knows there's no hope for you. You're just attitude all the time." Angel laughed and lifted her chin high. "Which is why we love you."

Max's eyes narrowed into tiny slits as she glanced across the table at Angel. "Are you saying that because I'm black?"

Angel leaned forward and her face morphed. "I'm saying it because you're Max. Anthony wouldn't love you if you weren't all filled with piss and vinegar. I bet you probably spank him." Angel smirked and raised an eyebrow. "Don't you?"

"The man deserves a whipping, not a spanking. He's more than I can handle."

"Pssh. Bullshit," Izzy quipped. "You handle him just fine. The same way I handle James."

The table erupted in laughter. There wasn't a woman at this table who hadn't taunted her man. It was part of the fun. Even Joe. The man could be merciless, and I loved every second of it.

"Back to our original topic," Mia said as she glanced down at her watch. "What time do we have to go?"

"We have thirty minutes to finish the next round to still get there on time with traffic."

I turned the delicate stem of the martini glass in my hands and kept my eyes veiled because I felt guilty not being able to hang out with the girls. But I needed to see my husband. "I can't go, ladies. Sorry."

Izzy pulled out her phone, punched a few buttons, and lifted it to her ear. "Hey, brother. We're taking Suzy out tonight. Okay?" I glared at her, unable to hide my annoyance, but she just stuck out her tongue at me like a child. "Why don't you tell her so she doesn't think I'm bullshitting her?"

She held out the phone to me, and I snarled as I

took it. I loved Izzy, but at times, I also wanted to knock her on her ass for being so goddamn bossy. "Hey, baby." My voice sounded sugar sweet, but if I knew Joe, he could hear my aggravation.

"Sugar, go out with the girls for a while. I'll come get you around eleven and bring you home."

"I want to come home and be with you." I pouted even though he couldn't see my face, which earned me a smack on the hand from Izzy.

She mouthed, "Pussy," and I flipped her the finger.

"We have all night. You have a little girl time. I'll put the kids down to bed and ask Mike to stay here while I come and get you."

"Mike's there?"

"He's stopping by. He said he wanted to talk to me, so I figured Gigi and Lily could have a playdate."

My husband is the best one in the world. "All right, Joe. As long as you're okay with it."

"I'm happy you're taking some time for yourself. Love you, sugar."

"Love you too," I said before handing the phone back to a very smug Izzy.

"Thanks, bro. I'll make sure she behaves." Izzy winked at me. The last time she was supposed to make sure I behaved, strippers showed up and Joe and I almost ended. "Later," she said before hanging up. "Everything's set. Let's drink up. We have a party to get to."

"I don't think I should have another." I've never been a big drinker, but over the years I grew more accustomed to it, especially hanging out with this crew. Once they introduced me to the flavored martini, there was no looking back. "My lips already feel a bit numb. I think if I have another, I won't be able to see straight." I bit my lip, and just as I had said, it was tingly.

"Perfect," Izzy snorted.

Hopefully, in the hours between drink two and Joe picking me up, I'd sober up enough to enjoy a night with my husband.

I pulled up my proverbial big-girl panties and tossed back the last of my martini before dragging the second one in front of me. I deserved to let go a little.

"Can I take this off now?" I asked and started to tug on the blindfold that Izzy just happened to have in her purse.

Izzy slapped my hand away. "Stop that. It's not time to take it off."

I gritted my teeth, annoyed with not knowing exactly where I was, but it wouldn't be a night out with Izzy without a little blindsiding. "Does everyone have on a blindfold or just me?"

"The other girls do too." I knew she was lying as soon as they all started to giggle.

"Let's do this," Sophia said from my side.

I leaned over toward her voice and hoped I was close enough that she could hear me if I whispered. "Should I be scared?"

"Nah," she muttered. "I promise you'll have a smile on your face soon enough."

"I'd better or I'm beating you after I beat Izzy."

A door opened and the vibrations of a musical beat in the distance caught my attention. Without my sight, my other senses became more acute. "Are we at a club?" I asked as Sophia's body moved before she opened her door.

"You can say that," Angel replied in a strange voice.

After climbing out of the car, I held on to Sophia's arm and walked on shaky legs. Martini number two hadn't been my friend. My entire body felt like jelly. I wasn't even sure my words came out without a slur, but I was so relaxed that it didn't really matter either.

The crunching of the gravel under my feet made it even harder to walk. "I'm taking this shit off," I whined and tried to remove the blindfold, but I almost lost my balance.

"No," Sophia jerked her arm, causing me to stumble further.

"Don't do that!" I yelled, grabbing on to her with both hands. "Are you trying to kill me?"

Sophia laughed. "We went through a lot of trouble for tonight. It's a surprise, so don't ruin it."

"Fine," I mumbled, and I didn't know if I should be flattered or scared.

"Good evening, Ms. Izzy," a man with an unfamiliar voice said as soon as we stepped inside.

The music wasn't completely audible yet, but the bass from the song made my insides rattle. I pulled Sophia closer. "Where are we?"

"Shh," Sophia told me.

"Good evening, ladies," he greeted us and his voice said he liked what he saw.

"These are my sisters, Master Kurt."

"I like sisters. I've always had this fantasy—"

"They're all married and off-limits," Izzy told him.

"Sure. My apologies. I'd hate to anger Master James."

Master James. I gnawed on my lip, trying to gauge my drunkenness, and trying to see through the blindfold but failed.

"The entire top floor has been reserved for your party. The rest of your group is waiting for you, li'l one."

"Thanks, Master Kurt."

Where the fuck am I? My stomach began to knot as we started to walk again, this time toward the music and the wicked beat vibrating through my system.

"We should go," I said when we stopped walking. I knew exactly where we were—Hedonism—James and Izzy's club. "I can't be here without Joe."

"Oh, hush. This is going to be the night of our lives. One for the record books, in fact." Max was somewhere in front of me, but I couldn't tell exactly where.

"There's no turning back now," Mia said as an elevator dinged and we began to move again.

"Fuck," I hissed and felt like I was about to expel the entire contents of my stomach, which consisted of exactly two martinis and nothing else.

When we stepped inside, the walls were rattling from the sexual beat of the music. Instantly, I regretted wearing a sundress with no underwear. I'd thought I'd surprise Joe when I got home from *one* drink with the girls. I'd figured I'd attack him on the couch and show him just how much I loved him.

Now, with nothing underneath, all I could think about were handsy men on a dance floor trying to cop a feel, getting more than either of us bargained for.

When the doors opened, there was an unmistakable scent in the air—sex. I shuffled my feet, moving apprehensively, and ready to kill Izzy for whatever her pea brain had concocted. Everyone with me tonight was on my shit list. They went along with her plan, knowing full well I would flip my lid.

A door creaked and Sophia led me inside. I swallowed down my fear, believing that my *sisters* wouldn't put me in harm's way or end my marriage.

"You wait here," Sophia said, pushing me downward.

Putting my hands underneath me, I felt for a seat and tried to relax. "Okay. Blindfold?"

"Leave it," Izzy commanded from a distance.

"Don't move." Sophia chuckled and patted me on the shoulder. "I promise it will be fine," she whispered. "Trust me." After giving me a light squeeze, the sound of her heels faded as she walked toward the door and closed it.

Besides the sound of Nine Inch Nails's "Closer" in the distance, the only thing I could hear was my heart beating wildly in my chest. My palms began to sweat and I tried to dry them on my sundress, smoothing it down in the process to cover as much of my body as I possibly could.

Swallowing down my fear, I sat perfectly still and listened for the approach of someone but heard nothing. I couldn't. The sound of my heart racing and the blood rushing through my ears drowned out everything around me except the erotic beat of the music.

When the door opened and slammed closed, I gasped.

CHAPTER 9
STAKING MY CLAIM
JOE

"I THINK there's been some mistake," Suzy said, looking pale and terrified as she sat on a stool in the middle of the dimly lit room, unaware that it was me who walked through the door. "I need to go."

"Shh." I took a step closer and her body moved backward.

"Please." Her hands gripped her knees so tightly that her knuckles started to turn white.

"I won't hurt you." I changed my voice just enough that I hoped I didn't give myself away and took another step.

"I'm married. I can't be here."

When she started to stand, I moved quickly, placing my hand on her shoulder and holding her in place. She gasped again as her bottom touched the stool. "My husband will kick your ass."

I'd actually bury a man for doing far less to her

than making her sit back down on a stool. She held down the edge of her dress, and I could see the tension in her jaw.

"Why didn't I wear panties?" she mumbled to herself, but not quiet enough that I didn't hear. My poor Suzy—she always had a way of saying the worst thing at the most awkward time.

"Ah," I moaned.

"No!" she shouted, shooting straight in the air.

Before she could take a step, I grabbed her arm and our bodies collided. Without giving her a second to hit me, I pressed my lips to hers and tasted the remnants of her favorite martini—cupcake. She pushed me away, smacking me across the face with amazing aim for not being able to see.

Just as her knee went up, about to get me right in the balls, I grabbed her leg. "Sugar!"

"Joe?" she whispered and stilled with her leg still in my hand.

"Yeah." I chuckled and let her leg go.

"What the hell? Why are you here?" Her finger looped into the side of the blindfold, ready to remove it, but I stopped her.

"Leave it," I told her, pulling her hand down to my lips. "I want you on edge tonight." I brought her body closer to mine and let her feel my hard-on.

Her lips found their way to mine, lingering just out of reach. "Thank God you're here."

I kissed her mouth and held her tighter. "Of course."

Her lips vanished as her head jerked back. "I was scared."

"I'm sorry, sugar."

She gasped. "Wait! Oh my God! Can people see us?" Her head turned side to side as if she was trying to see her surroundings.

I brushed a stray hair away from her face and tucked it behind her ear. "No one can. It's just us in this room."

"Oh."

"I plan to violate you tonight."

Suzy wrapped her arms around me and touched the bristle on my cheek with her tiny fingertips. "Was this *always* the plan?"

"Always. No more talking for you." I dragged my finger down her jawline. "We're going to do a little role-playing. You only speak when I tell you to, got it?"

"Well, um, I don't—"

"Shh, just let me have a little fun with my beautiful wife." She nodded and I kissed her again, happy that she didn't have a reply.

With our lips still connected, I moved backward until the back of her knees hit the lightly padded table in the middle of the room. "Don't be scared," I told her against her mouth. "I promise not to let anything bad happen to you. I'm going to make all your dirty fantasies come true tonight."

She didn't speak—probably too fearful, or maybe her mind was in overdrive and filled with lust.

My hands found the hem of her dress, pulling it slowly over her head. Noticing that she hadn't worn panties made me smile. She'd planned on getting lucky tonight, but I'm sure this scenario never entered her mind. "Lean back and lie flat." She slowly reclined, squirming a bit and fidgeting, while I helped her lie flat on her back. Surveying the room, I took in all the implements and toys that James had gone over with me before the ladies arrived. It made my stomach turn because I knew that kinky fuck had probably used half this shit on my sister. I tried to block it out and focus on their purposes and decide which ones I'd use on Suzy.

The dim lighting of the room and the sound of the music thumping through the entire building had my adrenaline pumping. Maybe it was seeing Suzy naked, lying on a table and waiting for me to do with her as I wished. My cock was rock fucking hard, and I prayed I could hold out long enough to have a little fun before I had to sink myself deep into her.

"Joe," Suzy whispered, facing the direction I moved.

"Just relax." I could tell that she was nervous and that I'd have to do something to keep her from fidgeting through everything I had planned. Without hesitation, I grabbed the restraints from the wall. James had shown me how to secure them under the table and restrict her movement.

I wasn't new to them. We'd played at home. Suzy always loved them. Usually, we used handcuffs Thomas gave me, but being unfamiliar with Hedonism's gear made it necessary to have a brief lesson. I wanted to make sure that if anything happened, I'd be able to free her easily.

"I'm going to tie your hands up." Her lips parted and she sucked in a breath as I walked closer. "It's just like at home."

She nodded and placed her hands at her sides. One by one, I secured them in the black, fleece-lined cuffs before clipping them together under the table. Her feet were tied to the table legs, and her wrists were connected to pieces that tied in a loose knot under the table…just not loose enough for her to get out.

She adjusted, testing her bindings before licking her lips. Her tits jutted out in that position, her legs far enough apart. The table wasn't like any other I'd ever seen. The bottom half came apart, letting the person in charge spread their submissive's legs for easy access. Plus—this was my favorite part—there was a latch under the head of the table that could adjust the person's head position, which made "face-fucking"— James's term, not mine—easy.

Honestly, I could see the allure of all this shit. But

instead of coming to a club, I'd love to have one of these in my bedroom. There were endless possibilities and fun that could be had with this piece of furniture.

"Joe," Suzy whispered when I reached for the flogger I had already set up on a rollaway tray next to the table.

"Yeah?" I asked, fisting the leather handle and turning it to get a feel for the weight. The last thing I wanted to do was strike her flesh too hard.

"Can we just do it regular?" she asked, catching me totally by surprise.

"You can't possibly mean that." I shook my head. We went to a lot of trouble to set up this entire evening for Suzy and all of our women. We wanted to make their fantasies come true.

I liked kink.

Fuck, I loved everything that had to do with having sex with Suzy, but I wanted to go above and beyond.

She loved her books, mostly the ones that dealt with BDSM. Over the years, we tinkered with role-playing and Master/slave in the bedroom. I'd never thought about bringing her to a club. I'm not into sharing, and I feared I'd have to pound someone's face into the ground if they even looked at her wrong.

"I mean," she sighed and bit down on her bottom lip. "I want to look into your eyes tonight. I need that connection."

I knew what she wanted—she liked it deep.

Wanted me to penetrate her to the point that I stole her breath. Sometimes she'd look into my eyes with so much intensity that I felt her love and need. "Anything you want, sugar."

This night wasn't about me. No matter how much planning we put into it and cash we threw at it, this night was about her and only her.

"You could leave me tied up, though, but I want to see your face."

I chuckled quietly to myself. Suzy always loved to be tied up. Without another word, I leaned forward and slid the blindfold off her head. She blinked slowly, letting her vision adjust to the lighting as she searched for my face.

As soon as her eyes found mine, the biggest smile spread across her lips. "Hey."

"Hey yourself, sugar."

Her head turned and she surveyed the room, taking in all the implements sprinkled about until her eyes landed on the tray of goodies I had planned for the evening. "Oh my God! You were going to use all that?" she asked with wide eyes, looking between the toys and me.

I rubbed the back of my neck and couldn't hide my smirk. "That *was* the plan."

"Fuck," she groaned, smacking her head onto the padded table. "That looks like a good time."

"I don't need all that—" I used my chin to motion toward the tray of toys as I started to unbutton my jeans "—to have a good time." Pulling my hardened cock from my pants, I fisted it, stroking it while I took a few steps toward Suzy. "Just you." Before she could speak, I released the latch between her legs and spread the table, and her legs, wide open.

"Oh my God!" Her head lifted off the table with wide eyes.

"I know." I couldn't contain my excitement, or my cock, for the matter. There was nothing sweeter in this world than sinking into her and becoming one.

Her pussy glistened in the light of the candles lining the walls. Ever since the babies were born, she hadn't really been interested in sex. I didn't push the issue either. We had enough shit on our plate, and she had enough going on in her mind that there was no way I'd push her into doing anything. When she asked for me to touch her, I did. Otherwise, I took care of myself and gave her time to heal.

Before this moment, I wondered when her sex drive would come back. I didn't know if it was the drink, the club, or me, but she was finally wet simply by my presence.

My pants were a problem because of my boots, but I moved them far enough down my legs that they wouldn't be in the way. "You want this?" I asked, stroking my cock through her wetness.

"Yes." She smiled and blinked slowly.

"I've been dying to crawl inside you for months, sugar." As I pushed inside of her, my eyes closed, the feeling of heaven almost overcoming my ability to think. "There's no sweeter place in the world than being inside of you."

"Joe." She moaned as I pushed deeper inside, her back arching off the table. She pulled on the restraints, trying to touch me, but she was trapped.

"Just lie there. I want to remind you who owns your body."

"You do." Her reply was swift.

"I do. Look at me, Suzy." I paused with my dick deep inside of her, swirling my hips to hit the one spot she loved. "Who owns mine?"

"I do," she said, gasping for air when my hips switched motion. "Oh God."

"That's right, sugar. You like that, don't you, dirty girl?" Resting my hands on her thighs, I spread her wide and gave myself more access...deeper penetration.

She grunted, bearing down on my cock, and gasped, "I do."

At this rate, I knew I wouldn't last long. I could count the number of times I'd been inside her the last few months on one hand. It was time to take matters into my own hands and get her off quickly before I let myself come. Leaning over her, I grabbed the small bullet vibrator that I brought from home off the tray.

When I turned it on and placed it against her clit, her entire body jolted. Her legs strained against the restraints and she tried to straighten her legs, but it was no use. I wasn't letting her out, and I wasn't about to stop. She didn't really want me to either.

"Don't stop!" she moaned, her hands contorting at her sides as her body grew rigid and her pussy clamped down against my cock.

I grunted, unable to form words. I was lost in the pleasure of her beautiful pussy and craving the release I so badly needed. As I thrust deep inside of her, over and over again, her body began to shake and glisten in the light. When she started to suck in air in short, quick intervals, I knew she was about to come. Just as her mouth fell open and she held her breath, I let myself sink into the blissful abyss of ecstasy.

Collapsing on top of her, I had reached…heaven.

CHAPTER 10
LIFE IS STRANGER THAN FICTION

SUZY

AFTER WE DRESSED and talked for a little while, we finally left the room. Before we walked out, I'd had an image of what Hedonism looked like in my head, but it was completely and utterly wrong.

It was nothing like I'd read in my books. There were no dungeons or dark corridors that led to salacious sex rooms. There were private rooms where couples could play. I had just had one of the best orgasms of my life inside one to prove it.

Hedonism was more like a nightclub, with the loud music, women dancing on pedestals in the middle of the room without any clothing, and a bar in the middle of the room. "This is it?" I looked up at him after I took it all in.

"Yeah, babe. Your books are bullshit."

"But… But…I pictured it differently." Where were the whips and chains, the St. Andrew's crosses, and the rest? *There had to be more.* "I refuse to believe this is it. There's no way this place is just a nightclub with private rooms for screwing." My eyes roamed over every inch of the space and honed in on Izzy, sitting at the bar with James. I grabbed Joe's hand, dragging him with me, and headed straight for her.

"Hey," Izzy said with the biggest smile when she saw me.

"Listen, this can't be all there is." I pushed back the few strands of hair that had settled on my shoulder. "I've been listening to you talk about this place for years. I'm a little let down, Izzy."

"That's on another level." She pointed down and smirked. "Jimmy and I rarely come up here. This is for the more vanilla crowd that just likes to watch."

Peering over my shoulder, I saw James and Joe giving each other that look...like I was asking for trouble. "Watch what?"

"Have you looked around?"

"Well, no." I rolled my wedding band with my thumb.

"Just look, Suzy." She pointed toward a dark area in the corner. A crowd had gathered, but I couldn't see a thing. "May I?" she asked James, and it caught me so off guard that my head snapped in her direction.

"Yes, you may." James had a different demeanor in this space. He wasn't the sweet, playful man I had grown to love. There was a presence to him.

Something had shifted between them inside this building. Izzy had explained their relationship to me many times. I'd read enough about Dominance and submission, but I could never picture Izzy being able to submit to anyone…even James.

"Come on." She yanked on my hand and led me toward the group in the corner. She leaned in, speaking quietly in my ear. "Look."

My eyes followed hers. On the other side of the crowd, there was a couple lying on a bed, surrounded by sheer curtains. But they weren't having a drink. They were fucking each other's brains out with everyone watching in fascination. The man had her on all fours and was pounding into her so hard I wondered how she'd be able to walk when it was over. We used to fuck like that, but with kids, it became not as common.

"That's enough for you," Izzy said and touched my arm. "Breathe, little Suzy."

"Shut up, Iz. Give me a minute." I was transfixed by the rhythm of the music and the movement of their bodies… It was like watching the best porn in the world.

"I never would have taken you for a watcher." She bumped her hip into mine and chuckled softly.

I batted her away and took a step closer, shutting out the world. I don't know how long I stood there watching before there was a tap on my shoulder. "Let's go, sugar. That's enough for you tonight."

"But, Joe, do you see this?" I pointed toward the man still pounding into her like a beast. I didn't know what he was on, but there was no way any human could screw as much for as long as he did without dying.

"I do." Joe shook his head but smiled. He wasn't judging me, and I wasn't embarrassed at my gawking either. "Do you want to see the other floor?"

My head snapped up, forgetting all about the sex scene in front of me. I felt like a kid at Christmas. "Really?"

"Izzy and James got us a visitor's pass. We're only able to watch and can't participate in any way."

"That's okay." I leaped into his arms out of sheer excitement. "This is the best day I've had in a long, long time, baby."

"I knew you were a freak, princess."

"You did this to me." I nuzzled my nose against his before peppering his face with kisses.

Izzy and James approached, and my mouth gaped open bigger than it had been before. Izzy had her collar on, which she never took off, but this time, there was a leash attached to it.

"What the what?" I whispered in Joe's ear.

"Don't ask. I'm going against everything I believe in to get you to see the club. Don't remind me of what she looks like."

"But she has a—"

"I know." Joe turned with me still clinging to his

body. My eyes fell back on the couple on the bed and the beast of a man still thrusting into her with Herculean effort.

"Sorry about this, Joe," James said, unable to look him in the eye. "There are rules on that floor. Izzy's my sub and has to either crawl at my side or be leashed."

Joe's jaw tightened. "Let's not talk about it. We're ready."

I inched down Joe's body and turned to face Izzy. She didn't look like the scary, kick-ass girl I knew. She looked like a woman under the thumb of her Master and completely in love. I kind of envied her. She gave herself to James. I had given myself in a way to Joe, but he didn't truly own me. Not in the same way James did Izzy.

———

I stared up and watched the fan as it rotated, casting shadows against the ceiling. My mind was still filled with the images from the club. It was everything I dreamed and more.

"Did you like tonight?" Joe asked from my side.

I turned and took in the beauty that was my husband. "I did. It was just so…" My voice trailed off because I couldn't put into words exactly how I felt.

"I know." He sighed and pulled my body closer. "Do you want to go there again?"

I bit my lip because the thought of it secretly gave me a thrill. But when I walked out of the doors at Hedonism, I said good-bye and knew I'd never step foot inside there again. "No. It was a fun night, but I don't think it's a place I could go again."

He propped himself up on one arm and stared down at me, his eyebrows drawn downward. "Why? I could tell it turned you on."

I swallowed down my momentary embarrassment because Joe knew I had a kinky side to me. "It's just not my scene. I love reading about it, and seeing it once was amazing, but it's not someplace I want to go on a regular basis. It's not me, Joe." My fingers found his face as I traced the line of his jaw. "It's not us."

"We can be anything we want. All I want is for you to be happy. I'll do anything to make that happen."

I smiled up at him, more in love than I think I ever had been. "I'd rather not go there. I can never be your sub. Although I like you being bossy in the bedroom and when we role-play, I'm not ready to have sex in front of strangers."

"Thank fuck," he groaned, smashing his lips into mine. "I don't want to beat the fuck out of someone for staring at your body. I don't know how James fucking does it."

"Different strokes for different folks." I giggled because I said stroke and instantly forgot my age.

"Actually, I don't want anyone to see your perfect body. I'm not into sharing you, love."

He hovered above me, staring into my eyes with lust. "Although, I regret not following through on my plan now."

"Tonight was perfect." Though his plan—based on the items on the tray—would've been amazing, I realized sometimes things were better left imagined than realized.

"Are you sure? I can get James to get us back inside."

I shook my head and looped my arms around his neck. "All I want is you. Nothing else. Nothing more."

He smiled down at me with softened eyes. "How did your last appointment go? We haven't had time to talk about it."

"Really good. I know I was pissed when you wanted me to go talk with her, but she really helped."

"I can tell she helped you with everything. It's just nice to have my sugar back."

"I was always here. Just a little lost for a while."

He crawled between my legs, settling his body weight on top of me. "I'll always be there to rescue you, my love. No matter what happens, I'll be there to catch you when you fall."

"I'd never expect anything less." Wrapping my legs around his waist, I could feel his hardness against my middle. I kissed him, drowning in him for a little while.

Joe had tried to make my fantasies come true tonight. But the thing he hadn't realized was I already lived them. The day I met him, everything in my life changed. Never did I imagine having a man like him and three beautiful children. Life was perfect. Months ago, I didn't feel that way.

I'd felt like I was spiraling down a black abyss without an end and unable to have the happiness touch me. After many therapy sessions and lots of love from my husband, I felt like I was finally able to see the little joys in life.

My children were beautiful and healthy, my husband was as devoted and loving as ever, and I couldn't ask for more.

CHAPTER 11
FULL HOUSE

JOE

"WE'RE HERE!" I yelled when we walked through the front door of my parents' house on Sunday afternoon. Each hand held a baby carrier with sleeping bundles of joy, while Suzy walked hand in hand with Gigi.

"Gigi!" Lily screeched from the living room and came barreling into the foyer to usher her away.

Sundays had become harder the larger the family grew. Babies weren't as portable as one would think. So instead of doing it every week, we'd changed to biweekly for the sake of our sanity.

"Let me take Ro," Suzy said and grabbed her carrier from my hands just as Rose's eyes opened.

"I'm going to put Lu down in the other room where it's quiet so she can sleep a little longer."

I headed to the den, which was now more like a nursery with the influx of babies in the family. If I didn't know better, I'd think my mom put something in the sauce each week to have us reproducing at breakneck speed.

When I opened the door, James was sitting in the rocking chair, holding Trace—their newest addition—and feeding him a bottle. Izzy found out she was pregnant just after we announced the twins. I don't know who she pissed off upstairs, but they gave her another boy. James was over the moon about it and Izzy was too, but she craved a girl so badly that I almost felt sorry for her. She deserved a girl—someone to drive her as crazy as she drove us—a cute little spitfire who matched her propensity for getting into trouble and stirring up a shitstorm

"Hey, buddy." James smiled at me, giving me his familiar chin lift. "Was afraid I wouldn't see you here today."

"Why?" Placing Lu near the bed, I sat down and stared at her while I enjoyed the last moments of peace I'd probably have the entire day.

"Just thought you and Suzy would take the weekend to reconnect."

I couldn't hold in my laughter. "If we reconnected any more this weekend, my dick would probably snap clear off."

"That good, huh? You guys going to come back?" He looked hopeful, but the thought of seeing my sister as his submissive again made me want to hurl.

"Suzy said she had a great time but it's not her scene."

"I get it. At least you gave it a shot."

"I'd do anything for that woman."

"Not to change the subject, but Thomas and I need to leave early today. We have some business to take care of before shit gets out of hand."

My eyebrows shot up. "What's up?"

James laid Trace on the bed behind me, asleep and in a milk coma. "He asked me not to say, but I'll tell you when we know more. Shit isn't good, but hopefully we're wrong."

"Fuck," I groaned and rubbed the back of my neck. "I thought things had been too damn quiet."

"Don't tell Suzy. They'll all start talking and ask too many questions. It's best to wait until they're apart."

"Gotcha." Suddenly the smell of meatballs and sauce didn't have my stomach churning out of hunger, but out of angst over what Thomas had to discuss.

I checked on Lu one last time before we closed the door behind us and headed into the living room. "Where are the ladies?" James asked as he took a seat on the couch next to Thomas.

"Kitchen." Thomas pointed over his shoulder. "Did you tell him?" he whispered.

"Tell him what?" Izzy asked, walking back into the room so quietly that neither of them heard her.

"Nothing. Man shit, babe." James tried to cover his tracks. "Some things are best as a surprise."

Izzy wrapped her arms around his neck, standing with her chest to his back as she leaned over the couch. "Some of us don't like surprises, Jimmy." Her hands groped his chest through his shirt. "Especially me."

James looked to me for the rescue, but I sat down across from him and kept my mouth shut. There was no way in hell I was getting involved and becoming the subject of Izzy's questioning.

Thomas peered over his shoulder at Iz. "I need their help with something. Nothing major, sis. Just need a little muscle."

"Uh-huh." Izzy eyed him cautiously but let the subject drop. "Dinner will be ready in five."

All the guys in the room stared at the television and waited for her to get out of earshot.

"You dumbass. You almost blew it." Thomas elbowed James in the ribs.

James scrubbed his hand across his face. "Fuck, I didn't hear her come up behind me."

"No more talking about it. Just come when we call." Thomas's eyes scanned the room as he waited for silent acknowledgment of his statement from each of us. "I'll give Morgan a heads-up since he couldn't make it tonight."

"How's Morgan anyway?" I asked because I hadn't seen our cousin in weeks.

"Good, just busy with Race and the new business. Their weekends are sucked up with the track and getting everything working like a well-oiled machine."

"Good for them," Anthony finally joined the conversation after putting his phone down. "Max is going to have my balls when we meet for leaving her at night with the kids."

"Want me to talk to her? You know she has a thing for me." Mike laughed and flexed his muscles, kissing each bicep.

"Dinner!" Mia yelled from the kitchen and saved Mike from getting a punch in the face from Anthony.

"Lucky son of a bitch," Anthony grumbled when he walked past Mike and headed toward the dining room.

Just as I was about to follow, I heard Lu start to wail from the den. Turning on my heels, I went to grab her before taking my seat.

"Hey, princess," I said when I reached down into the carrier and scooped her into my arms. "Couldn't wait ten more minutes for Daddy to have dinner?" She cooed and lifted her leg, her hands finding her feet and playing with her toes.

Suzy walked in, carrying a sleeping Ro in her arms. "We can swap them out. Let me just put her down and I'll grab Lu from you."

"Babe, I got her. You just relax at dinner and eat. I'll hold her in my lap."

Suzy gave me a lazy smile after she set the baby in

the carrier. "Have I told you lately how much I love you?"

"Every day." Moving to her side, I grabbed her hand and gave it a little squeeze before leading us into the dining room.

"Sal, we're going to need a bigger house." Mom gave Pop the eyes, which usually earned her anything she wanted, but typically, her requests were small.

"Someday, Mar. If these kids keep having babies like they're trying to repopulate the world, we'll have no choice but to get a bigger place." Pop laughed before he scooped the biggest heap of pasta onto his plate.

Mom glanced around the table. "I think it needs to happen soon, because I think there's going to be more Gallos."

"Don't look at me." Izzy waved her hands wildly. "I'm getting fixed. Three boys are enough for me."

"But you need a girl," Ma replied.

"Nope."

"We're done too," Max added and elbowed Anthony.

"Yep. No more."

"Oh, there's always room for more babies. More kids means more love."

"You've been saying that forever, Ma. But more kids means more dirty diapers, sleepless nights, and sexless days." Mike chuckled and gave Mia a side glance as she was cutting Lily's meatball into tiny pieces.

"You're a jerk." Izzy smacked him in the arm. "Like you have ever changed a poopy diaper."

I loved my brother, but the simple fact that changing a diaper made him weak in the knees made me question his manhood. You couldn't legitimately call yourself a father unless you stepped up to the plate and took part in everything.

"Don't listen to him. He's so full of it. Literally," Mia said and rolled her eyes. "The man has changed more than his share of diapers. He just likes to pretend like he's too big of a man for that, but he's been covered in crap."

"We are trying to eat." James gagged. "I have enough baby crap to wade through on a daily basis."

"Ma seems to forget all the bad parts of being a mother since she wants us to have more babies." Thomas pulled the bowl of meatballs in front of him, but he didn't dare look at Ma. "She wants more, but she gets to pop in and out of their lives while we're stuck with baby puke and volcanic poop."

"You kids act like I didn't go through this with all of you. I did, and it's part of being a parent. I never complained when I would play with you and you'd puke on me. I didn't whine when you crapped the bed."

"That was Mike." Thomas laughed and pointed at him.

"Eff you. I was sick."

"Sure," Anthony teased him, and Mike looked like he was about to jump over the table.

"It's just what we do. If I didn't go through all of the bad things, I wouldn't be sitting here today with a table full of you and all the love I have in my life. I love your father, but if it were just him and me, I'd go crazy."

"True," Pop said and leaned over, kissing her cheek.

"When you're older and your kids are grown, you'll forget all the sleepless nights, dirty diapers, and other things that make most people cringe. You'll be thankful to be surrounded by your kids and loved ones. So stop your complaining and eat."

My head jerked back. Ma was a little tougher on us than she usually was, but I think it was only because she wanted more grandkids. If she had her way, we'd have double the amount than sat in this house.

I glanced over at Gigi and thought about Ma's words. There wasn't a day, no matter how rough it had been, that I ever regretted having her in my life. She meant the world to me. She was forever a tiny piece of Suzy and me walking this earth. We'd never be forgotten as long as she was around.

CHAPTER 12

CHANGE IS IN THE AIR
SUZY

GIGI TOOK after her aunt Izzy more than me. Sometimes I looked at her and knew that the Gallo genes won out in my womb when she was created. She had their dark skin, warm brown hair, and attitude.

Ro and Lu, the twins, were an even mix of both of our families. They had sandy blond hair, light eyes, and ivory skin. I prayed every day they wouldn't have the Gallo attitude, which often led to trouble.

"Mrs. Gallo, sorry I had to call you to the office today." Sitting in the principal's office, even as an adult, made me weak in the knees.

Even when I was a teacher, the very mention of a meeting in the principal's office brought back memories of my childhood and being scolded for my behavior.

"I completely understand, Ms. Wisen. What did Gigi do to warrant this meeting?"

"Would you like to wait for your husband?" she asked.

The woman looked like she'd be a hard-nosed principal, but I didn't think that could be the case for any elementary school administrator. You couldn't surround yourself with the smallest, innocent creatures and not have a warm heart. Even though she was dressed in a dark suit, she had on colorful rubber bracelets for various school fundraisers from the school year.

"He couldn't get away from work. It's just me today." I'd been here before. Gigi had been in trouble on other occasions, typically for using profanity she learned from the Gallos. They had loose tongues, and kids were quick to mimic the language of those around them.

"Ahh, he's a tattoo artist, right?" Her nose wrinkled.

"He's a business owner, yes." I glared at her, feeling disgust at her presumption about him based on his artistic profession.

"Well, there was an incident this morning that has many teachers concerned here at Spring Elementary."

I fidgeted with my hands and tried to remain calm. I'd been in this office for more nonsense than I ever imagined possible. "What kind of incident?"

Gigi was a good kid. She did have some of her aunt in her personality, but she was never malicious or cruel. It was starting to feel like a witch-hunt and Gigi was the target.

"She told a boy that he was only hers and then tried to kiss him."

I smiled, unable to hide it, because she sounded like her father and me. The apple didn't fall far from the tree. Actually, she sounded like every Gallo with those words. She'd heard them many times growing up.

"Is this funny, Mrs. Gallo?" Ms. Wisen sneered at me with disgust.

"She's just a kid. It's cute that she has a crush."

Wisen needed to lighten up. She probably hadn't been laid since Bill Clinton was in the White House. Kids did stuff like this all the time. I remember cornering my first crush and giving him a kiss, probably against his will since boys often thought girls were gross until puberty kicked in.

She clasped her hands on the desk in front of her. "It borders on sexual harassment."

My mouth fell open at the ridiculousness of it all. "You can't be serious. They're children."

"This is how it starts. It's a slippery slope from here."

I rolled my eyes. "Ms. Wisen, I'll speak with Gigi about not touching others, especially kissing them.

She won't do it again, but in no way is it sexual harassment."

"We have a very strict no-touching policy here at Spring."

"It won't happen again."

"What's more concerning is her language. Telling the boy that he was hers and only hers. He was in tears this morning."

Clearly his parents didn't use that language at home. "She didn't mean anything by it. She's heard it said by many members of our family. It's harmless."

"I don't know what kind of unhealthy relationship you have at home, but that type of expression is not acceptable."

I stood quickly, smoothing my dress before leaning over her desk. I was done with her insinuating there was something wrong at home for Gigi to act the way she had. "There's nothing wrong with her father and me. We love each other. We're committed to each other. Maybe if you had someone as devoted to you as we are to each other, you wouldn't find the language so disturbing. I'm sorry your life is so bland and boring that claiming someone as yours is out of your realm of comfort, but I can assure you that it's not meant in a negative way. I'll speak to Gigi about touching others, but there is nothing wrong with her or our family. If you continue to single her out as an issue, I will take you to court for harassment. Just try me, Ms. Wisen. I've worked in education for years. I know how it works, and once you target a child as an issue, every small thing they do can be picked out and used against them. You need to leave my child alone and pay more attention to the real problems in the school."

The fucking bitch. I could feel her attitude and disdain for Joe and me before she even began speaking. Maybe I was wrong. Wisen wasn't a teddy bear at all. She was a frigid, prude of a woman who needed to get fucked six ways to Sunday.

"There's no need to get lawyers involved, Mrs. Gallo."

"My husband may be a tattoo artist, but we are in no way poor. If you mess with my family again, I'll sink every dollar I have in my bank accounts into ruining you. Do you understand me?" On the outside, I appeared calm and collected, but my insides were shaking. Not out of fear, but in anger.

She held her hands up in front of her in a defensive manner. "Understood. I didn't mean any harm."

"Saying my daughter is sexually harassing someone is just being an asshole. I'm taking Gigi with me for the rest of the day. I'll share the incident with her father and let him decide how to handle the situation." I stuck my purse under my arm and straightened my body. "It'll be entirely up to him. I don't know if he'll be quite as kind as me with his words either."

Without a backward glance, I marched out of the office and slammed the door. That earned me a look of shock from every person sitting in the office waiting. My hands shook as I texted Joe and told him we'd discuss what happened at the school tonight. I already knew he would be more pissed off than I was, but I'd figure out a way to calm him down. I always did.

"Hey, Mommy. Why are you so mad?" Gigi asked, placing her hand in mine after she walked into the office.

"Some people aren't very nice, Gig."

"I know." She tugged on my arm so I'd lean over. "Ms. Wisen is the meanest there is too," she whispered in my ear but not quiet enough not to be overheard.

"I know, baby. Daddy will deal with her." I smiled because the busybody office ladies would pass that on to the evil Ms. Wisen.

Gigi backed away so I could see her face with widened eyes. "Oh, is she going to get spanked like Daddy does to you?"

I bit my lip, hiding my laughter and feeling my face heat with embarrassment. "Not quite like that, Gig. I see we have to have a long talk about Mommy and Daddy. You've heard too much, baby."

"I hear it all, Mommy. *You've been a bad girl.*" She mimicked Joe's voice, and I wanted to wipe the words from her mind.

"Come on. Let's go get some ice cream and talk about what happened today," I told her before lifting her into my arms to get out of there as quickly as possible before she said something else.

"We gotta talk," I said to Joe when he walked through the front door after work.

"Wisen?"

"Yep. And a few other things Gigi said today." Standing on my tiptoes, I kissed him on the cheek before nuzzling my nose against his five-o'clock shadow.

He shook his head and smiled. He knew the things that could come out of her mouth, and usually, he was pretty proud of his little spitfire. "What did she say now?"

"Well, for starters…" I led him by the hand to the couch and pushed him down by the shoulders. "She told a boy today that he was hers."

His head fell forward. "Jesus, isn't she too young for this shit?"

I kneaded his shoulders, trying to relieve some of his tension while using him as a human stress ball. "She's just acting out what she's seen at home."

"Shit, I hope not."

"That's another thing."

"What is?"

"It seems that Little Miss Gigi overhears us."

"I know. She's mentioned things to me that she shouldn't know about."

My hands stilled against his rock-hard shoulders. "So you knew?"

"Yeah, she said some things to me months ago and I forgot." His body started to shake under my fingers when he began to laugh.

"Well, today she wanted to know if you were going to spank Ms. Wisen for being a *bad girl* just like me."

His laughter grew louder. "It's kind of funny, no?"

"I'd be laughing if it weren't so embarrassing." The very thought of it still made me want to puke.

"She has no idea what it means."

"Especially since she never gets spanked." Neither of us believed in hitting our children. It was a line we'd never cross. Gigi had to be confused why I got spanked but she didn't. There was no way in hell I'd explain it to her either.

"I'll talk to her. Why did Gigi want to know if I was going to spank Wisen? What did that bitch say now?" A low growl came from him, his body vibrating under my hands.

"She said that Gigi's behavior bordered on sexual harassment."

He turned around and faced me without a single ounce of humor left on his face. "She can't be fucking serious."

"She was." I started to work my fingers again and tried to get him to relax. "Don't worry, I put her in her place."

"I want to know everything that happened."

I spent the next hour discussing with him the ramifications of Gigi's actions and how Wisen felt our home life might be unhealthy for a child. By the time we were done talking, Joe was more pissed off than I thought he would be. If I were Ms. Wisen, I'd be worried. Hell hath no fury like a papa bear protecting his little cub.

CHAPTER 13
PAST COMES BACK TO HAUNT

JOE

THOMAS TEXTED me before I left work to gather my brothers and meet at ALFA before going home. We were under strict orders not to share the meeting with Izzy.

When I pulled into ALFA at eight sharp, the rest of the gang was already there and waiting. There was something gnawing at me about this meeting. If it was no big deal, Thomas would've talked about it at my parents' house. But since he called a special meeting, there had to be something he didn't want the rest of the family to overhear.

The front office was deserted except for Thomas, who had waited at the door for me. After I walked inside, he looked around outside before locking the door and escorting me down the hallway.

"What has you so freaked out?"

"I'll explain once we're in the conference room,"

Thomas answered before pushing open the door to a full room. Around the table sat James, Anthony, Mike, Sam, Morgan, Bear, Frisco and Tank. This wasn't just a group—it was an army.

"Thanks for coming, everyone," Thomas said before taking a seat at the head of the table with me at the opposite end. "I know I didn't give you any details, but there's something I need to share with each of you, and we felt this was the best way to do it."

We all leaned forward, silent, and ready to hear whatever Thomas was about to announce. I could tell by the worry in his eyes and his paranoid behavior at the entrance that he wasn't about to announce good news.

"I just received word that a few of the members of the Sun Devils MC have been released."

"What?" Sam asked, slamming his fist down on the table. "How is that even possible?"

"Some technical bullshit. Their lawyers have been working tirelessly on appealing their convictions."

"How many?" Frisco asked and rubbed the back of his neck. "I need to know what we're dealing with here."

"One, possibly two members, max." Thomas leaned back in his chair, rocking nervously.

I closed my eyes and tried to control my rising blood pressure. I knew when he finished his *assignment* with the DEA and the Devils were behind bars that it would never truly be the end. "Now what?" I asked, opening my eyes and staring straight at Thomas.

"I want everyone to be extra vigilant and careful. If there's anything suspicious, the rest of the group needs to know. I've been assured that they're unaware of who I am or that I was part of the DEA—the same for James and Sam—but we can't be too careful."

"You think they haven't figured it out?" Mike asked as he rubbed his temples with his head resting in his hands.

"I can't say for sure. Even though the agency has assured us that they haven't, we can't be certain. I know information passes easier than many people think inside prisons, and if they have enough ears and eyes out there, they know that I never went away."

"Fuckers," James snarled with clenched teeth. "We're going to have to kill every one of those pricks to keep our families safe."

"Fucking hell," Anthony added and looked up at the ceiling like it held the answers to save all of our asses.

"I'm ready," Morgan said and cracked his knuckles.

"I worry that they'll come after anyone in my family. Not just Angel or Izzy, but any one of you around the table, along with your wives and kids."

"I knew you should've never worked undercover." Mike's veins were protruding from his forehead. No doubt he was getting a headache at the mere thought of all the shit that was about to go down, just like I was already thinking about at length.

"While I gather some intel this week, just keep your eyes out for anything out of the ordinary. We can't take anything too lightly. We don't know if they've figured out who we are and if they're already watching us. Understand?"

"Yeah," I said, clenching my fists tightly on top of the table, wishing that the motherfuckers were in front of me right now. I'd have no problem ending them to save any person around this table or in my family... even Sam.

"We got it," Anthony added. "I'll keep the girls close."

"Nothing will get by us," Tank said, looking around the table. "You guys are the only family I've got. I'll have your backs."

"Don't tell the girls yet. We don't need them in a panic."

"Oh, sure, you hold a secret from Mia and see how that pans out for you," Mike whined and tipped his head back, scrubbing his hands across his face.

"Better to be a whiny Mia than a dead one. Got me?" James told him, and Mike's head snapped forward.

"Got it."

"We'll know more in the next few days, but I need to know that you'll report anything unusual. And I mean anything."

"What if they come after one of us?" Anthony asked what we were all thinking.

"Then we do everything we can to protect our families. Keep them close, everyone. Keep the guns loaded and ready. The Sun Devils are some crazy bastards, and they aren't above killing innocents."

We walked out, stunned and in complete silence. When I climbed into my car, I sat there for a moment and thought about the possibility of losing someone I loved. I'd never let it happen. There wasn't one person close to me for whom I wouldn't jump in front of a bullet to protect. Whatever happened, I knew everyone else felt the same way.

No matter what... we'd protect what was ours.

CHAPTER 14
SOMETHING'S OFF

SUZY

EVER SINCE JOE came home last night, he's acted weird. At first, I thought maybe it was because of what happened with Gigi and school, but that couldn't be it. Maybe spending time at Hedonism wasn't the best thing for us. I thought we were in a better place.

"Baby, what's wrong?" I asked, wrapping my hands around his waist as he looked out the sliding glass doors overlooking the backyard.

He patted my hands and gave me the brushoff. "Nothing, sugar. Just thinking about work."

That shit was a lie. One he used often. I even called Izzy to see if there was something going on at Inked that would have him worried. She said everything was fine on the shop front. When I asked her if James was acting weird, she said not any more than usual.

I buried my face in his back and inhaled his scent, the one I'd loved so much since the first day I met him. "There's something you're not telling me, Joe."

"There's nothing, Suzy. Stop worrying. Nothing is wrong."

But even though he said the words, I could tell his voice wasn't full of conviction but of something else, though what I wasn't sure.

"I'm meeting Mia for lunch today. Your mom is going to watch the kids so we can hang out."

He turned in my arms and my cheek rested on his chest. "I don't think that's a good idea."

I stared up at him with confusion on my face. He'd never said no to me. "Why not?"

He wrapped his arms around me and rested his face against my hair. "It's fine, just be careful."

"When am I not? It's not like something is going to happen. It's just a quick bite to eat at Grillz." My stomach rumbled at the thought of the food. They offered every type of grilled cheese imaginable, and it had quickly become the go-to spot in the city.

"Fine." He kissed my head before something caught his eye in the backyard.

"What is it?" I asked, turning quickly to see what he did, but there was nothing.

"Just an animal, sugar."

I released him. "I'm going to get the girls ready and head out for the day. Need anything?" He was already typing furiously on his phone and not paying any attention to me. "Joseph, I'm talking to you."

He didn't look up or make any effort to stop his conversation. "What? Sorry, I didn't hear you."

I didn't even bother to ask him again. What was the point? Whomever he was texting had his attention, not me. After I dressed the girls, we headed to Grandma's house for their visit and my time with Mia. I needed some girl time...a little time to share my feelings with one person I knew wouldn't utter a word to anyone.

Something was going on, and I needed another person's opinion on how to proceed. Mia was one of the smartest, most level-headed people I knew. Maybe I was making something out of nothing, but in my experience with Joe, that wasn't usually the case.

CHAPTER 15
REALITY VS. IMAGINATION

JOE

WHEN SUZY LEFT THE HOUSE, I headed straight to ALFA. I could've sworn I saw something or someone in the woods behind my house, but I couldn't tell if it was just paranoia creeping in or reality.

Thomas hadn't given us a full update since we had our meeting last week. Information had come in via text and was limited.

"Hey! Sit." Thomas shuffled papers around on his messy desk. "I really need to have Angel organize all this shit. It's out of control."

"Maybe if you stopped sticking your dick in her during business hours, she'd get more work done."

He laughed and shrugged. "Sometimes I can't help myself. You try working with Suzy all day and resisting her."

"You're a sicko."

"No argument here."

"So what's going on with the Sun Devils? I swear I saw someone in the woods behind my house this morning."

His demeanor changed instantly. "Are you sure it was a person?"

"I can't say for sure, but something was out there. I felt like whatever it was, it was watching us."

"I spoke with my contacts at the DEA. They lost track of a few of the members." His fist slammed down on his desk. "They're good for nothing."

"Have you noticed anything out of the ordinary? It could've been an animal and my mind playing tricks on me. I'm so fucking on edge that I could've made the entire thing up."

"I haven't noticed anything, but I know exactly how they are. I'm more worried about the people I care about than myself."

"We need to know more, Thomas. Everyone needs to know what's going on. You need to get more information as quickly as possible and share it with us."

"I'll find out more today and get the guys together for a quick meeting tonight around seven. Good?" He picked up the phone and pressed a button. "James, get Sam and come to my office, please."

"It'll have to be. I'll let the guys know. You just find out the info. We can't be left in the dark if our lives are in danger."

Using both of his hands, he rubbed his temples and sighed. "Hopefully, tonight we'll know enough to get a plan together to keep everyone safe. I refuse to let them rule our lives and hurt anyone we love."

"Maybe they'll take Sam as a sacrificial lamb." I grinned because he'd pissed me off since the day I learned that he and Izzy had a thing.

"Don't be an asshole. You know we need him." He shook his head and rolled his eyes.

"Maybe you do."

"He came in handy before. Remember he did take a bullet for us."

It was my turn to sigh. "Fine. We won't offer him in exchange for our safety. We'll figure out another way."

"What are we exchanging?" Sam said from the doorway.

It was my cue to leave. "I have to get to work. See you tonight at seven," I told Thomas before turning to face Sam and James. "See you guys tonight." Pushing past them, I nudged Sam just a little bit.

"Fucker," he muttered.

"Sit. We have some shit to talk about," Thomas said before the door closed.

As I walked to my car, I took in my surroundings and looked for anything or anyone that didn't belong. Nothing seemed out of place. I chalked up this morning to an overactive imagination and fear.

Nothing usually scared me… But the thought of

the Sun Devils coming for the people I loved had me on edge. By the time I pulled into Inked, my nerves had calmed and I felt more at ease than I had since I saw movement in the woods.

"Yo!" Mike greeted me at the door. "Where have you been?"

"I ran to ALFA for a bit to talk with Thomas."

Mike's face morphed and grew serious. "What's up?"

I placed my hand on his shoulder, giving it a light squeeze. "I don't want to talk about it here, but we're meeting tonight at seven."

"I'll be there and I'll text Anthony to let him know too."

"Where's the lazy bastard?"

"With Max at the doctor. It's her yearly checkup and ataxia evaluation. Dumb fuck," he said before punching me in the shoulder hard enough that my body rocked backward.

Guilt flooded me. "Shit, I forgot."

"Way to go, champ. Way to be a douche."

"Who's a douche?" Izzy asked as she walked into the front of Inked, wiping her hands with a paper towel.

Mike thumbed toward me over his shoulder. "Joe."

"Usually, it's you being a douche, Mikey. It's nice to have someone else at the helm for a bit, isn't it?"

I pushed past Mike, shoving him off-kilter in the process. "Fuck off, Iz. I don't need your shit today."

"Someone pissed in your Wheaties this morning, didn't they?" Izzy laughed, tossing her hair over her shoulder and following me toward the back.

"I just have a lot of shit on my mind."

"It seems to be the norm around here. If I didn't know better, I'd think your cycles are in sync."

"Cycles?" Mike plopped down in Anthony's chair and started to leaf through the latest issue of *Tattoo* magazine.

"You're like a bunch of chicks...all PMS'ing at the same time."

"That's sick, little sister."

"All of you have been grouchy as fuck for a week now. I want to gouge your little eyes out and sew your lips shut." She closed one eye and pretended to be doing just that from a distance.

"We put up with your cranky ass our entire lives. We're entitled to a few days out of the year." I started to prep my station for my first appointment of the day. It was a back piece and would suck up most of my shift, but it was completely worth it to see the finished product.

"I know something's going on. Even James is acting weird. Suzy called me the other day and asked me a few things that had me curious too. So, what gives? Spit it out, boys." Her eyes moved between us while she waited without saying a word.

When neither of us replied, she said, "I'm talking to both of you. I want answers."

"There's nothing going on, Izzy," I told her with the straightest face I could because she always seemed to know when we were bullshitting her.

"Michael?"

He cleared his throat and hunkered down below the top of the magazine. "Nothing at all."

"You bitches are hiding something, and I'm going to figure it out. When I do…you're going to be sorry."

I turned my back to her, grinding my teeth together. I hated hiding stuff from her. I hated doing it to anyone in the inner circle. But knowing Izzy like I did, she'd go off half-cocked and get all the ladies riled up and cause more problems than she'd solve.

When we finally sat down at the conference table at ALFA that night, I heard the words I'd been dreading come from Thomas's mouth. "They're in town and they're looking for us."

I no longer believed it was an animal in the woods outside my house, but someone watching us—someone lurking in the shadows, waiting to strike.

"Goddamn it," I growled.

"They're not getting through us," Morgan said, slamming his hand down on the conference table.

"We need to come up with a plan to keep

everyone safe." Bear put his hands together and rested them against his lips. "One that requires killing anyone who gets near them."

"We have to tell the girls," James groaned and dragged his hands down his face. "They're gonna flip."

"Break it gently." Thomas stood and paced in front of the table. "We need to have protection on the women at all times. From here on out, our lives change until we're in the clear."

"You need to stay out of sight, brother," I said with my jaw clenched tightly.

"I'll do no such thing." He shook his head and picked up the pace. "I'm the bait. We have to draw them out. If I stay hidden, this may never be over."

"You're right." I grimaced at the though of dangling him out there as the sacrificial lamb. But he was right, he was the only way to get them to show themselves.

By the time we left AFLA, we had a plan in place. It was time to alert everyone to keep them safe. We spent all night forming a plan to do just that…for us all to get out alive.

CHAPTER 16
NEVER A DULL MOMENT
SUZY

I SAT down on the lanai, holding homemade lemonade, and put the phone on speaker. "I just don't understand how you let him lead you around like that." It was my favorite spot to do some thinking when the house was quiet and I was alone.

"I know you've read books about it, Suzy. Come on. You know how it works."

"Oh, I know exactly how it works. But my question is, how do *you* do it? I mean, you're so damn bossy, I can't imagine you taking any shit from James." The sound of the animals moving through the woods drew my attention. They were more active tonight than usual.

She laughed. "I top from the bottom all the time."

"I'm sure you get your ass beat for doing it, too."

"Ahh. I do. That's half the fun."

"But aren't you embarrassed being led around on a leash? I don't know if I could do it."

"I'm not embarrassed. I would be if we walked around the grocery store like that, but at the club, it's normal. I like being his and letting everyone know it."

"I don't know if I'll ever get that image of you out of my head."

"Girl, you know I could bring that man to his knees in a heartbeat."

"Kicking him in the balls doesn't count." I chuckled because I knew James loved her, but he was the boss in the household. He was the only man I'd ever seen "handle" Izzy.

She started to laugh. "Fuck, I have to go. Trace's awake and crying for me."

"Love you, Iz."

"Love you too, Suz." The phone went dead.

I stared off into the darkness, listening to the twigs snapping, and my stomach began to knot. Whatever was creeping in the woods wasn't small. Maybe it was already gator-mating season, something I had come to learn was really a thing in Florida. They were more active, walking farther to find a mate. It was the only time of year that I'd sometimes check under my car before daring to get inside.

After I finished my lemonade, I went back inside and headed upstairs to check on the kids. Lu and Ro were sound asleep, each in her own crib as stars moved across their ceiling and soft music played. For the first few months of their lives, we kept them in the same crib, not wanting to separate them after being smooshed together in my womb. They had grown fast, in true Gallo style, and could no longer fit comfortably in one. Plus, they were waking each other up, and I couldn't take any more sleepless nights.

I brushed Ro's hair back and whispered, "Mommy loves you," before heading to Lu's crib and doing the same. I walked backward quietly on tiptoes out the door, before closing it and heading straight for Gigi.

She'd been a trooper. Since the babies arrived, she'd become the best big sister. She loved helping me take care of the babies. She'd often say they were "hers."

"Mommy," Gigi said in the cutest little girl groggy voice as I sat down on her bed.

"Go back to sleep, baby girl." I rubbed her cheek with the back of my fingers. She still hadn't lost that baby softness to her skin. "I love you, buttercup."

"Love you too." She rolled over, facing away from me. Softly, I rubbed her back and hummed her favorite lullaby until she drifted back to sleep.

I couldn't believe I'd been so lucky. My life was blessed and perfect. When I thought back to the time I met Joe, I'd never imagined my life would turn out this way. I almost didn't give him a chance. The very thought of not having him or my girls in my life made my heart ache. They were everything to me.

"Take a seat, sugar." Joe rubbed the back of his neck, pacing around the living room like a caged animal after he arrived home from a secret meeting at ALFA Investigations.

"Okay," I said, my voice drawn out and light. He never acted like this, never talked to me in that tone, unless something was wrong. "What's wrong, babe?" When my bottom touched the couch, I put my hands in my lap and tried to ready myself for whatever was coming next.

"There's no easy way to say this." His eyes were filled with fear as he ran his hands through his hair. "But I don't want you to freak out."

My belly plummeted. He couldn't honestly be serious. "I'm already freaked out."

Every horrible scenario started to go through my mind. Was he having an affair? Maybe he was leaving me.

"You're in danger."

I hoped he didn't want a divorce. I couldn't imagine being a single mom to three kids.

"We're all in danger."

My head snapped back, his words finally making it past my wild imagination. "What?" I looked up at him, confused and caught completely off guard.

He sat down next to me, holding my hands in his as our knees touched. "Thomas has it on very good authority that some of the members of the Sun Devils MC may be looking for him."

"Oh, God," I whispered and closed my eyes. "I thought they were in prison." My eyes fluttered open and I looked at my husband, trying to hide my terror.

"They were, but some of them have recently been released, and they're looking for Thomas. They're probably looking for Sam and James too, but Thomas for sure."

"I can't believe this." My voice cracked and the words lodged in my throat. "How is this possible?"

"It's fucked up." His thumb stroked the soft skin on top of my hand, rubbing the same spot over and over again.

"Do they know who he is?"

"It seems they do." He glanced up at the ceiling before his cheeks filled with air, puffing out before he exhaled.

"But how? I thought the government would protect him."

"Everything can be bought for a price, sugar, even names."

My eyes began to fill with tears. I never thought we would be in danger. My naïveté over how the government worked had me walking through each day with blinders. "So they're coming after all of us?"

"I don't know." His body reclined into the couch, and I took the opportunity to crawl into his lap.

"What do we do now?" I said, tucking my head under his chin and resting my cheek on his chest.

His hand stroked my back. "We need to be very careful for now."

"Am I going to be a prisoner in this house?" My fingers traced the outline of his pec.

"No, sugar. You won't. We just need to make sure the doors are locked at all times, the kids aren't outside alone, and that we keep our eye out for anyone near the house. When you aren't home, just be conscious of your surroundings. If someone looks out of the ordinary, you need to let me know and make sure not to be alone."

My finger found its way to his nipple, toying with his piercing underneath his shirt. "Maybe it's time I learn to shoot a gun."

"Fuck," he muttered into my hair.

Pressing my palm flat on his chest, I pushed myself up to look him straight in the eyes. "You're not always home, Joe. I want to know that I can protect the girls if someone comes in the house."

His hand snaked around my neck and his thumb rested on my cheek. "You're right. We'll go to the range tomorrow."

"I'll never let anything happen to the girls, baby."

"That's what I'm worried about." He blew out a breath and shook his head slowly. "I never want you to be in a situation where you have to shoot someone."

"Joe," I said, nuzzling my nose against his. "I know you worry, but it's best that I can defend our family if need be. You can't be here all the time. I want to know that I can handle any situation on my own. I'll feel better about being here during the day when you're out or at night if you stop by the Neon Cowboy."

"I'll be going to work and coming straight home. I don't want you to be alone longer than necessary. No more Neon Cowboy unless you're with me. No more guys' nights out."

"No?"

His eyes shifted. "There will be no more girls' nights either."

"Hold up there, buddy." I placed his face in my hands, much in the same manner Gigi did when she wanted to get her way. "We're not *allowed* to have a girls' night out?"

"Not out. You girls can meet at one of the houses where it's safer." His eyes came back to mine. "Okay?"

Resting my forehead against his, I caressed his cheeks with my fingertips, feeling the scruff that had formed throughout the day. "We'll figure something out."

"No harebrained schemes either. It's too dangerous right now."

"Fine," I whispered.

"Suzy, I'm serious."

"I know." I wouldn't go against his wishes, especially if our lives were in danger. Izzy, I wasn't so sure about. She'd be harder to control. The image of her with the leash and James spanking her ass popped into my head, and I started to laugh.

"What's so funny?"

"Nothing."

"Suzette, you can't keep things from me. Not now."

"Well…" I sat up and smiled. "I was thinking about how James was going to control Izzy through this. I thought about her at the club with the leash—"

He put his hand over my face. "Do not ever speak of that night again," he said with wild eyes. "I've wiped it from my mind."

"It was sexy, though," I mumbled into the palm of his hand.

"It's my baby sister. If I didn't know her so well or like James so much, I would've knocked his lights out." He pulled his hand away, and I bit my lip to stop from smiling again.

"You wanna play slave and Master?" I asked, quirking an eyebrow.

"As long as I get to be the Master." He grinned and my belly flipped.

I squealed and bounced in his lap, feeling his cock harden underneath me. "I'll never say no to that." My husband needed to get his mind off things. I wanted to get lost in him and not think about the people who might be after us. I'd do anything to give his mind a moment's peace.

After I climbed off his lap, I turned around and wiggled my behind in his face, which earned me a slap on the ass.

"Strip," he commanded before I could take another step.

I froze, glancing up the stairs. "But the kids."

"Are they sleeping?" he asked as he stood.

"They are."

He crossed his arms over his wide chest, placing his feet shoulder-width apart. "I didn't think slaves were allowed to speak."

"We haven't started yet."

"I'll give you one reprieve. As soon as the bedroom door closes, you're mine, sugar."

"You got it," I said as I dashed up the steps before he could catch me.

"I'm waiting," I whisper-yelled into the hallway from the bedroom door. "Are you man enough for all this?" My hands traveled up my body as I swayed my hips. I probably looked like a moron, but to Joe, I was the most beautiful girl in the world.

"I'm ready for everything I plan to take." He closed the bedroom door, grabbing me by the waist and carrying me to the bed. "Where do I begin?"

"I've been a bad girl." I smirked, knowing I was in for it, and I couldn't have been more excited. Joe Gallo was all mine.

walked to the dresser. He opened a drawer and took a ... pistol out.

He aimed it at me ... the ... he ... it ...
... away ...
and my ... him ... in the ... behind me ...
... down the stairs.

"Stop," he commanded, something ... I took a ... step.

"Don't glance up the stairs. Got it?"

"Are they up?" I asked ... he ...
"They are ..."

He crossed his arms over his ... with ... playing ...
his feet shoulder-width apart. I didn't think there were allowed to speak.

"Where ... are they?"

"I'll give you one chance ... as soon as the bathroom door closes, you ... hurry, ..."

"You ... I can't ... running the steps below her and could not ...

"In a line," I whispered into the hallway ...
... the bathroom door. Are you ... enough for all those AK ... maybe ... up my body is ... my finger ... ... looked like a ... but ... love ...
... most beautiful in the world ...

This was the everything I didn't ... take ...
gave the bathroom door ... pushing ... by the door and carrying me to the bed. What do I mean,
"Perhaps I had gel," I murmured ... kisses in ... and I couldn't give to his ... then ... for ...
Gallo was all mine.

CHAPTER 17
IT'S ALL IN THE WRIST

JOE

"THAT'S IT, SUGAR." The thought of her having to use it on someone made my skin crawl. "Just point, aim, shoot."

"That was fun," she said with her earmuffs still in place. They had pink ones at the range for the ladies, and she looked cute as a button and scary as fuck all at once.

"It's not supposed to be fun."

"You're such a Debbie Downer," she said when she set down the Glock 19.

I placed my hands on her shoulders. "It won't be fun if you have to kill someone."

She wrinkled her nose. "No, that would be horrible. But I'd do it if I needed to, Joe."

"Always aim for the chest. It's easier to hit."

"Gotcha." She nodded and removed her earmuffs. "Last resort. Point, aim, and shoot at their chest."

"Right." I wrapped my arms around her and pulled her close against me. "Don't let the person get too close. You don't want them to get control of the gun."

"Okay," she sighed before squeezing me tightly. "Want to go to lunch?" She batted her eyelashes at me, knowing full well it was hard for me to say no.

"I can't. I'm going to be late for work. Want to come with me, and maybe after my first client, we can sneak away? I'm sure everyone would love to see you."

"You sure Ma will be okay watching them a little longer?" She looped her hand behind my back as we walked out of the shooting range.

I threw my arm over her shoulder and tucked her under me. "I'm sure Ma is happy as a pig in shit right now. She'll be fine."

My mother would be in her glory surrounded by her grandkids. Her house had almost become like a day care. Kids were shuffled in and out every day. Slowly, she had amassed an army of Gallos and still wanted more.

I climbed onto the bike, straddling it between my legs and waiting for Suzy to jump on back. Every time she rode on the back of my bike, I thought about our first night together. She had been so afraid of riding with me. Now, when shit got crazy, she asked me to take her for a ride so she could feel the wind blowing through her hair. Times had changed.

"Suzy!" Izzy screeched when we walked through the front door of Inked. She blew past me, nudging my shoulder in the process, and headed straight for my wife.

"Good morning to you too," I mumbled before walking to the back and leaving the girls alone.

"Yo," Mike said like he always did every morning when he saw me.

I grumbled instead of replying. He was a little too happy for me this morning.

"Brought Suzy with you today?" He glanced toward the waiting room before looking at me again.

"Yeah. We were at the range."

"Golf?" His head jerked backward and his forehead wrinkled.

"No, dumbass. The shooting range." I started to ready my station—laying out plastic wrap over everything to make the area sterile and avoid a ton of cleanup later.

"Ah. How did that go?"

"Better than I thought, actually."

"What went better?" Anthony asked when he walked out of the back room.

"Joe took Little Miss Suzy to the shooting range."

Anthony's eyes grew wide. "Holy fuck!"

"Don't start."

"The thought of Suzy with a gun scares the fuck out of me. And it's eerily sexy too."

"Don't let her hear you. She'd probably shoot you in the balls," I told him, even though we both knew it wasn't true.

"That cream puff?" he laughed. "The person who should never own a gun is our little sister."

"Too late," Izzy said when she walked into the back with Suzy close behind her. "I own more guns than all of you put together." She smirked and placed her hands on her hips. "I've got great aim too."

"You're not allowed to count James's guns into your total."

"We're married. What's his is mine and what's mine is mine."

Mike gave Izzy a weird look. "You can't have everything, Iz."

"Watch me," she said, tossing her hair behind her shoulder and walking toward the storage room.

"Clearly you still aren't well-versed in the way of the woman, Mikey," Suzy said with a giggle as she took the open chair to my left.

"Mia loves me." He shrugged.

"You better hold on to that one, brother."

"Fuck you," he said, flipping me the middle finger.

"Want to get anything pierced while you're here, Suzy Q?" Mike asked, glancing at me briefly with a wicked grin before turning his attention to the appointment book.

"I heard clit piercings are amazing."

I choked. "Absolutely not!"

"Don't knock it until you try it," Mike teased as he turned the page. "I have some time to fit you in."

"She doesn't need your services."

"Joseph," she said with a voice so smooth and calm that I knew I was about to get yelled at, but she could say anything she wanted… Mike was not going to be looking at her naked. He'd seen enough when he pierced her nipples years ago.

"I think I'll get my balls pierced, then." I didn't bother to look at her while I placed the inkwells on the table.

"Don't you dare! I love your balls."

Mike started to gag. "I don't want to think about your junk."

"I love your pussy, sugar. No one touches it but me."

"All right, all right." She put her hands in the air. "I don't need anything pierced today, Mike, but thanks. I don't wear my piercings anymore. Not since Gigi was born."

"Seriously?" He glanced at me before shrugging. "Just trying to be a helper."

"If you really want to help, why don't you go organize the back room? It's a bigger mess than usual." Izzy walked out, carrying some new bottles of ink we received yesterday to restock the stations.

"We've been so busy with all the other shit that I haven't had time." He dragged his hand through his hair, looking much like myself lately—stressed. "Mia freaked out when I told her last night."

"Why didn't you assholes tell us sooner?" Izzy asked, glaring back and forth between them.

"We didn't want to say anything until we knew for sure."

"I don't know how James expects me to live in a bubble. I have shit to do, people to see, and places to go. I can't have a bodyguard looking over my shoulder and following me around like a puppy dog."

"A bodyguard?" Suzy asked, leaning forward in her seat and putting her face in her hands.

"James said he's going to assign a guy from ALFA to each of us until it's over." Izzy rolled her eyes.

"What?" Suzy shot up from the chair and fisted her hands at her sides.

"He called me this morning with that brilliant idea. Idiot."

James had the right idea. We could defend ourselves, but our women needed extra protection, especially with the little ones running around.

"When?" I asked and felt a weight lifted off my shoulder.

"Starting tomorrow. He said they're going to close

any open cases and be assigned to the Gallo girls first thing in the morning."

"Oh, dear God." Suzy straightened, stiff as a board. "I don't need a babysitter."

"Hey, if you're lucky, you'll get one of the cute ones." Izzy's statement made me listen a little closer to their conversation. "Maybe Bear will protect you. He's a handsome devil."

Suzy blanched. "He's like a brother to me."

Thank Christ.

"Frisco?"

"Again, like a brother."

"Sam?" Izzy grimaced saying his name.

"Even Sam has become like a long-lost cousin."

"You realize I'm sitting right here, yeah?" I growled.

"Hush it," Izzy said, pointing at me. "You're hopeless. Babysitter it is."

"Damn it," Suzy said and collapsed back into the chair. "Do you really think this is necessary, Joe?"

I sighed, and even though my brother and James didn't always have the best ideas, this one was spot-on. "Afraid so, sweetheart."

"It's such bullshit," Suzy grumbled.

Everyone looked at each other in shock at her words, and I knew shit was probably going to be hitting the fan very soon.

CHAPTER 18
CAGED ANIMAL

SUZY

AT EXACTLY NINE in the morning, Frisco knocked. "Hey, doll," he said when I opened the door.

"Hey, Frisco. Come on in," I told him and stepped to the side for him to walk inside.

"Hey, buddy." Joe greeted him in the foyer with a giant smile. "Glad you're here."

I rolled my eyes because I wasn't happy about his presence in my home. I loved Frisco, we'd been friends for years, but that didn't mean I wanted him watching over me the entire day, every day, until the threat was neutralized.

"Just know I'm here until you get home, and I'll keep them safe." Frisco smiled and glanced at me out of the corner of his eye. "I know Sunshine isn't happy about this, but I promise to stay in the background and out of her way."

Without saying a word, I walked out of the room

and headed toward the kitchen. Ro and Lu would be hungry soon, and I was warming up two bottles and mixing some rice cereal for their bellies. The two girls ate way more than I ever remembered Gigi eating at the same age. They were growing like weeds.

They both were rolling over constantly and ready to start crawling. I dreaded that day. Right now, I could keep an eye on them because they stayed wherever I set them down, but as soon as they crawled, it would be a constant game of cat and mouse.

I looked around the living room, where I spent the most time, when Joe and Frisco walked into the room. "Babe, can you grab some baby gates today on your way home from work?" There were easily five ways for the twins to escape from this room.

Joe grabbed his keys off the counter and shoved his wallet into his back pocket. "What happened to the ones we had?"

"I gave them to Max to use. I want new ones anyway. Get at least five. Five," I repeated and pointed at each entryway. "I don't want to be chasing them around the house all day."

He wrapped his muscular arms around me, cocooning me in his warm embrace. "Gotcha. I'll grab at least five and more if they have them. That way we don't have to move them around the house."

"Thanks, baby." I stood on my tiptoes and kissed his soft lips.

"I won't be gone too late tonight."

"I'll be okay," I reassured him and peered over his shoulder at Frisco. "I'm sure Georgia will be happy if Frisco makes it home at a reasonable time." The statement earned me a wink from Frisco.

"No going anywhere without him. Got me, sugar?" Joe stared down at me with his stern look I loved so much.

"Whatever you say, Joe."

When I smiled, his eyes grew more serious, his stare turning more severe. "I'm serious. Do not go anywhere without Frisco."

"Yes, sir." I saluted him.

He smacked me on the ass before pulling me closer against him. "Don't make me punish you later."

Rubbing my nose against his, I laughed. "It's not really punishment when I like it."

Joe shook his head and sighed. "Be a good girl."

I tucked my hand under Joe's T-shirt and dragged my fingertips over the dimples above his ass. "Just go to work. I promise not to put my life in danger—or our girls. Stop being so overprotective and scoot. You're wasting Frisco's time, Joe."

"I'm out. Thanks for being here."

"Just go," I repeated myself, letting my hand wander down to his ass and giving him a small pinch. He barely flinched. He said good-bye and walked out.

I turned to face Frisco. "Sucks having to babysit me, huh?"

"I'm not babysitting you, Sunshine." His arms were crossed in front of his chest, muscles bulging under his solid black T-shirt.

"What would you call it?"

He laughed and tipped his head back. "Protecting you and the girls."

"Coffee?" I changed the subject, because what he called protecting, I called watching. "We have a few minutes peace left until Ro and Lu are up to eat again."

"Sure," Frisco said, unfolding his arms before walking toward the island counter.

He looked good. Better than I'd ever seen him. Being with Georgia, his wife and my good friend, agreed with him. Pushing them together was difficult. The two of them were so quick to find reasons not to be together, even though they were perfect for each other. They almost reminded me of Joe and me when we first hooked up.

"How's Georgia?" I asked, pouring him a cup of coffee.

"Working like crazy these days. There's some book fair at the school, so she's been staying late."

I always loved the book fair and missed being surrounded by so many new novels. "I miss the fair. Maybe we can stop in there this week."

"She'd like that." He nodded and took a seat as I pushed the mug in front of him. "Thanks, Sunshine."

After refreshing my cup, I leaned over the counter and stared at him over the rim while I took a sip. His hair was a little shorter than usual, probably Georgia's doing. His face had barely aged a day since I'd met him. That's what happened when you didn't have three little ones to wear your ass out. I felt like I'd aged twenty years in under seven. There were barely any wrinkles near the outer edges of his almond-shaped eyes. "Any plans for babies?"

He started to choke on his coffee. "Not yet. G's too young still." Using the back of his hand, he wiped his lips.

"That's the best time to start. You're not getting any younger."

"Thanks, Ma."

"How are your parents, anyway?"

He moved to Florida to escape them, but after his mother visited when he was dating Georgia, she decided to move closer to her son. She was a piece of work. She made Mrs. Gallo seem like a lightweight. "They're good. They're way too much in our business, but I know Ma's heart is in the right place."

"Does she like Georgia now?"

"It only took a year or so, but I think she finally accepts her."

"She doesn't think she's a tramp anymore?"

That earned me a laugh. "No. She realized the error in her ways."

"About damn time," I said before finishing the last drop of coffee in my cup. Just as I was about to speak, Ro started to scream upstairs. Before I could move, Lu joined in. "I gotta get them."

"Want help?" he asked, setting his coffee down and standing.

"I'm used to doing it myself."

"I have two free hands, Suzy. I'm not going to follow you around all day. I'm going to head outside soon to survey the perimeter, but I can help you carry the babies downstairs."

"I won't turn down the help." The girls were so heavy that, at times when carrying them both, I wondered how my back didn't give out. Especially when carrying them down the stairs. I hadn't thought ahead when we built the house. Why didn't we build a ranch?

Frisco followed me up the stairway and into the girls' room. "Shh, Ro," I whispered before pulling her from her crib. She was already waiting, holding on to the side for dear life and making sure to scream toward the door so I would hear her.

"Man, they're getting so big," Frisco said when he lifted Lu up and cradled her in his arms. She instantly quieted and peered up at him with wide eyes.

"They grow like weeds, my friend."

By the time we made it back to the kitchen, Lu

was cooing at Frisco and touching his face. His eyes lit up when he stared at her.

"You look good with a baby in your arms."

"Soon, Suzy. When Georgia's ready, we'll start our little army."

I handed him a bowl of rice mush for Lu and grabbed one for Ro before sitting down at the counter with him. "Just feed her small bites. Like this," I said, scooping some of the bland, colorless food onto the spoon.

"What about a high chair?" He stared down at her with a twinge of fear in his eyes.

"It's easier since there's two of us to just hold them. If you're not comfortable, you can put her in the chair."

"No. I can do this." He swallowed hard before repeating my motions and filling the spoon with food. "Just shovel it in?"

"Put it near her mouth and she'll open for you." I placed the spoon near Ro's mouth and she immediately opened. "See?" Lu's eyes sparkled as she stared up at him.

Frisco tentatively placed the spoon in front of Lu's face, but she opened for him without hesitation. "There you go, baby girl. Eat the nummies." Frisco had a paternal side. He just didn't know it. No one calls it that unless they have the baby talk down pat.

"She likes you." I smiled at them both.

He leaned forward and kissed her forehead,

lingering just a little to take in the baby scent. "She's a cute little thing."

I didn't have the heart to tell him that her cuteness would wear off soon. After she had her cereal and drained her bottle, she'd have her morning poop. Lu was great that way. Her body was like clockwork. I could almost set my clock to her morning bowel movement.

"So what are you going to be doing here all day?"

He gave her another spoonful, keeping his eyes on her as he spoke. "I'll be outside a lot. I need to make sure no one enters the perimeter, and since you have a lot of land, there will be a lot to cover."

"Don't stay outside too much. It's too hot to be out there long."

"I've been through hotter when I was on the battlefield, babe. We didn't get a break."

"Well, this isn't the military. Come in whenever you need something to drink or to just cool off."

"I will," he promised when he placed the last spoonful of cereal into Lu's hungry mouth. "Now what?"

"Bottle time." I nudged the waiting bottle toward him. "Want to go sit on the couch for it? It's just easier."

"Sure." Frisco grabbed both bottles in one hand, holding them between his long thick fingers and carried Lu with him to the couch. I followed behind with a fussy Ro and took a seat next to him. "Here," he said and handed me a bottle before adjusting Lu in his arms. When he stuck the bottle in Lu's mouth, she instantly started to drain it. "Jesus," he muttered as he stared at her with wide eyes.

"Yeah, they eat like they're starving to death."

"It's cute."

"Just wait." I giggled because I knew in under five minutes he'd meet the not so cute side of Lu.

We sat in comfortable silence, feeding the babies and enjoying the quiet time. Frisco had always been one of my favorite friends of Joe's. He quickly became my friend, and especially once he hooked up with Georgia. I knew he'd always have my back. I think I liked him the most out of the Neon Cowboy guys because he wasn't a perverted sicko like Tank and Bear, although they had their moments when I loved them too.

"What's that smell?" Frisco's nose wrinkled.

"Lu."

"Oh my God. How does something so horrid come from someone so beautiful and tiny?" His lips angled down and his face turned a funny shade of green. Big, bad military man couldn't take the smell of baby poop.

"Just be happy it's not climbing out of her diaper and soaking through her onesie."

"What?" He looked at me with wide, confused eyes.

"You'll learn someday, Frisco." I placed Ro in her

carrier and snapped her in before placing her on the coffee table in front of Frisco. "I'll change her, just finish giving Ro her bottle." I held the half-full bottle in front of him.

We swapped bottles and I lifted Lu from his arms, instantly hit by the stench. "Will she do the same thing?"

"No." I chuckled and glanced down at Ro. "She's more of an afternoon pooper. We still have a few hours until she clears a room."

"Thank God." He scooted forward to get closer to Ro.

"Men are such lightweights," I whispered to Lu when I carried her into the den, which we'd set up as a makeshift nursery so I wouldn't have to run up and down the stairs all day. "A little poop and they freak out. Not Daddy, though, he's like a pro." I smiled down at her as I set her on the changing table. She blew raspberries and grabbed her toes.

After I unsnapped her onesie and exposed the dirty diaper, I held my breath. "I wish I could keep you like this forever."

Someday she'd grow up, far too fast, and I'd have to deal with her teenage years. I couldn't imagine her old enough to have a boyfriend. Joe would probably be the one crapping his pants when his daughters started to date. It would be payback time for all the ladies he wooed in his youth.

"You're such a pretty girl," Frisco said in the cutest baby voice to Ro. "Just like your mommy."

I couldn't stop the smile on my face from growing wider. Frisco made me blush. He probably didn't know I could hear him, and I'd never embarrass him in that way, but it was nice to know that even after three kids had ravaged my body, I still had it.

After I cleaned up Lu, we headed back into the living room to find Frisco cradling Ro in his arms. "Couldn't help yourself, could you?"

"They need to bottle this scent. It's intoxicating." His nose rested on the top of her head as he gently rocked her back and forth in his arms.

"You're so ready to be a dad. Be careful, once you get the baby bug, it doesn't go away."

He exhaled and his shoulders relaxed. "I could do this." Just as he went to kiss her cheek, the little princess let out the biggest burp. Frisco gagged, probably getting a whiff of the baby formula that had already soured in her belly. "Maybe I need a little more time," he said, backing away from her and taking a deep breath of fresh air.

"You still have time." I giggled and placed Lu on the rug in the middle of the room.

"I better get outside. City would have my balls if he knew I was in here playing house."

"Probably right."

Ro looked like a newborn in his giant arms when he stood. He rocked back and forth on his feet, gently patting her back before he set her down next to her sister. "Thanks for a nice morning, Sunshine."

"Thanks for the help," I told him, before taking a seat next to the girls on the floor.

"Holler if you need me. Text if you hear or see anything, and I'll be inside before you know it."

I gave him thumbs up. When he walked outside and the door closed, I collapsed onto my back next to the girls and stared up at the ceiling. All I wanted to do was climb into a warm bath and relax. But mommy duties superseded everything else. Maybe in five years when the twins started school, I'd have a moment to myself again. Maybe.

Frisco stayed outside until late afternoon. I kept peeking through the curtains to check on him, but I'd barely catch a glimpse before he'd disappear again.

"Everything okay in here?" he asked after I let him through the sliding glass doors that lined the back of the house.

"Everything is quiet and calm."

"Good." He nodded and wiped the sweat from his brow.

I quickly grabbed a towel for him and a glass of water. "Sit down for a bit. You deserve a break."

He took the water and downed it before I had even had a chance to move. "Where are the girls?"

"Sleeping." I handed him the towel and took the glass from his hands to refill it.

"I've been thinking a lot about what you said."

With my back to him, I stared down at the water with my eyebrows furrowed. I couldn't remember what I'd said to him earlier. I was still half asleep and worn out.

"I think I'm ready to be a dad."

I whipped around, almost spilling the water in the process. "You are?" I couldn't stop my eyes from being as big as saucers.

"I am. Now to convince Georgia."

I tried not to jump up and down. I already knew she was ready. She had talked about it to me many times, but she worried Frisco wasn't ready. She didn't want to rush their relationship, especially since they were newlyweds.

"I'm sure she'll be on board. Talk to her about it. She may surprise you."

His face brightened. "You think?"

"I do!" I screeched and had to tell myself not to run to my phone and text Georgia the good news. Soon he'd be back outside and I could drop the bombshell on her.

"I think it's time we start a family of our own." His smile grew large and his shoulders went backward, puffing out his chest. "I'm ready for it."

The baby smell had gotten to him.

It gets everyone.

CHAPTER 19

SPANKS FOR THE MEMORIES

JOE

FRISCO TEXTED me every hour with a status update. Everything had been quiet on the home front, and nothing out of the ordinary had caught his eye. When I pulled into the driveway, he was waiting for me outside.

"Everything okay?"

He nodded and absently rubbed the back of his neck. "Yeah, everything is fine."

"Why do you look like you've seen a ghost, then?"

He dragged his eyes to mine. "I realized something today."

"And that is?" I twirled the key ring in my fingers, trying to keep my anxiety under control.

"I want a family. Spending time with Suzy and the girls has made me realize that I want that too."

I trapped the keys in my fist and laughed. "You

scared the fuck out of me." I punched him in the arm and shook my head. "You can be a prick sometimes."

"I'm being serious. I didn't think I was ready for kids, but now, I'm not so sure."

"You better be sure, brother. There's no return policy on a kid."

"I know." He hung his head and ran his fingers through his hair. "I'm going to talk it over with G and see what she says."

"Suzy's probably already told her you want them."

"What?"

"You know Suzy. She can't keep a secret. If you told her how you feel, I'm sure Georgia is already expecting the conversation."

"Fuck! I forgot she can't keep a secret."

"Yep." I laughed and glanced over his shoulder, noticing Suzy waving at me through the window.

"You're going to be a good father, Frisco." I grabbed his shoulder and gave it a light squeeze. "There are very few men that I can say that about, but I've known you long enough to know that any kid would be lucky to have you as a dad."

The unsure look on his face changed; his lips that had been set in a firm line curved into a big smile. "That means a lot coming from you, man."

"Now go the fuck home so I can spend some time with my wife."

He nodded and punched me in the chest. "Don't make another baby."

"Fuck you. I'm all about the practice." I laughed, pretending to pound into someone.

"I'd have thought you'd have figured out how to fuck by now." He shrugged and waved at me over his shoulder.

I flipped him off, but he didn't see. When he pulled away, I took a final glance around the yard, grabbed the baby gates out of the trunk and headed inside.

Suzy greeted me with the biggest smile and not much else. "I missed you today." The sheer, pink nightie she had on didn't leave much to the imagination.

"Did you have this on in front of him?" I held her at arm's length and took in her beauty.

"Are you crazy? I had my robe on, and he's been outside for the last hour. When I saw him pull away, I threw my robe over there." She pointed toward the white robe that had barely made it onto the couch.

"Sorry," I said and put my lips against hers. "I don't want any man seeing what's mine."

"Honey," she whispered. "There's no man I'd let see me naked besides you."

"Fuckin' better not," I growled. "So what's for dinner?" I didn't have the heart to tell her I had a burger at work because she'd probably spent all evening burning the shit out of something inedible.

She rested her hand in the center of my chest and looked up at me with a naughty grin. "Me."

I lifted her off the ground, smashing her tits into my chest and feeling the hardness of her nipples through my shirt. "Kids sleeping?" I asked against her lips.

"Out like a light."

Without another word, I tossed her over my shoulder and took the stairs two at a time. She squealed halfway up and I smacked her on the ass to remind her to quiet down. If she woke the kids, our fun-filled night would turn to shit in a heartbeat.

"How am I supposed to stay quiet when you smack me on the ass?"

That statement earned her another tap on her cute, perky ass. "Shush it, woman. Save it for when we're inside our bedroom."

"Promise to spank me some more?" she asked and massaged my ass cheeks with her small fingers.

"I plan to do more than that," I told her as I kicked open our bedroom door with my foot, but not hard enough to make it smash into the wall behind it.

As she slid down my body and her feet touched the floor, I said, "I think it's been far too long since I've felt your mouth on me, sugar. Be a good girl and I'll reward you for your efforts."

She licked her lips and glanced down at my already bulging hard-on. "I've been dying to taste you all day." Without hesitation, she knelt and started to undo my jeans.

I pulled my shirt off, throwing it on the floor across the room and readied myself for the feel of her lips on my cock. Although I loved being inside her, Suzy's mouth was heavenly.

The feel of her small, strong fingers wrapping around my cock made my body jerk forward. My dick led me out of instinct, wanting to be inside her more than anything in the world. When her tongue touched the tip, my eyes closed and my breath hitched. Even after all these years together, there was no other woman I could imagine being with besides my sugar.

Her velvety tongue slid against the underside of my shaft as her lips closed around my length, toying with my piercing. I felt drunk on lust and had to hold on to the wall for support before my knees gave out. She palmed my balls in her hand, moaning deep in her throat, causing the vibration to shoot straight to my spine.

I'd never been quick to come, but seeing her on her knees and sucking me off the way she was, it took everything in me not to make it over before it ever truly began. I cleared my mind and concentrated. It required all of my attention to focus on the tiny things —the scrape of her teeth against my flesh, the softness of her lips around my dick, and the flick of her tongue as it passed over my piercing.

I tangled my hands in her hair, needing her to slow down and wanting to savor the moment. "Slower, baby," I said, glancing down at her and almost losing it after watching my cock disappear between her lips.

Her mouth opened and she pulled back, holding my cock in her grasp. "You suck a dick and try to take it slow." She didn't stop stroking my shaft and playing with my balls as she spoke. "It's not the easiest thing in the world."

"Looks pretty easy to me," I replied and instantly regretted my words.

"You need to shut your mouth or you're just getting a hand job… That's if you're lucky."

"Sassy little thing, aren't you?" I smiled down at her, nudging her face back toward my dick.

"Want to spank me?"

The woman loved getting her ass spanked when I fucked her. She got off on it, and I loved every fucking minute of it. I never hit her hard enough to inflict real pain, just the right amount to cause a sting and remind her of where I'd been for the next couple of hours.

"Put your mouth back on me."

"Or what?"

"Or I'm not going to spank you." I grinned because it was a complete lie. I'd do anything she wanted. Anything to make her happy.

"In that case—" She wrapped her lips back around me and sucked with more vigor than she had before.

My eyes rolled back and my body lurched forward, chasing her lips. When I couldn't take it anymore, I pulled back and kicked off my pants. Before I could speak, she ran to the bed and got on all fours. "I'm waiting," she said, wiggling her ass in my direction and glancing over her shoulder with the cutest damn look on her face.

It was going to be that kind of night, and I couldn't be fucking happier.

When my eyes opened in the morning, Suzy was still in bed with me, staring down at me. "What's wrong?" I asked, my voice still gravelly from sleep.

Her hand slid down my chest, disappearing underneath the sheet. "I want to have a party for the Fourth of July. Is that okay?"

"I don't see why not." All sleepiness vanished when her hand wrapped around my cock.

"Because nothing would make me happier than to throw a huge party with all our friends and family." Her hand began to slowly stroke my length, causing me to harden in a few seconds.

"As long as you're happy, I'm happy."

"You know what else would make me happy?" she said, toying with my tip between her fingers.

"What, sugar?"

"If you got a vasectomy."

My hard-on disappeared.

CHAPTER 20
ALL IS FAIR IN LOVE AND WAR
SUZY

"WHAT THE FUCK HAPPENED THIS MORNING?" Izzy said over the phone before I could even say hello.

"Nothing, why?" I rested the receiver on my shoulder and stuck the bottle back in Ro's mouth before she screamed.

"He walked into the shop cranky as hell."

I bit my lip and felt a small twinge of guilt, but it quickly vanished. I pushed three human beings out of my body, the least he could do was get snipped so I wouldn't have to do it a fourth time.

"I kinda told him he should get a vasectomy."

She started to laugh—quietly at first, but it grew louder and verged on hysterics. "I can't believe—" She sucked in some air and kept laughing. "You're ballsier than I thought." She coughed, trying to catch her breath. "I give you a lot of credit, Suzy Q. As much as I'd like to, I don't think I could tell James to do the same."

"It's only fair, Izzy. I don't want another baby, and it's the least he can do."

"Oh, girl. I get it. I do. I get why he's all growly now. He's worried about his precious bits."

"It's not like they lop them off. He's not an animal. It's a simple cut and heals quickly."

"I know. I know. But you know how men are about their junk. You'd swear it was vital to survival."

"Well, if he still wants to have sex with me, he'll get it taken care of."

She started to laugh again. "I gotta go. My client just walked in."

"Izzy," I said quickly before she could hang up. "Don't tease your brother about it. This is between us."

"Yep. Sure thing," she replied before the line went dead, and I let the phone drop to the cushion next to me.

As soon as Ro finished her bottle, I put each of them in their carriers and texted Frisco that we were ready. I needed to get out of the house after feeling like a caged animal and trapped with the babies for a few days. We were only going to the grocery store, but I was happy to go anywhere.

"Are we going for a few hours or for a week?" Frisco asked while he shoved everything into the back of the SUV.

"There's no such thing as traveling light with kids, especially twins."

"I can see that."

"You need a stroller, bottles, diapers, and everything else imaginable in case something unexpected happens."

"Like what?" he asked, grabbing Lu's carrier from my hands before hoisting it into the back seat and snapping it into place under my watchful eye.

"Well, like one of them could have a diaper malfunction and could need a change of clothes." I locked Ro's carrier into the backseat and closed the door.

"Does that happen often?" His mouth gaped open.

I scrunched up my face when I climbed into the passenger seat. "More than you wish it did."

He rubbed his forehead before pressing on his eyes. "Maybe I need to rethink this baby thing."

"Did you talk to Georgia last night?" I had completely forgotten to message her and give her a heads-up.

He nodded slowly and started the engine. "Yeah. We had a long talk."

Pulling down the visor, I checked my makeup. "And?"

"She said she's ready to start trying."

"Oh my God," I squealed and clapped my hands like a crazy woman. "This makes me so happy."

He gave me a sideways glance. "Why do women get happy about that shit?"

"Because it means our babies can play together. Maybe you'll have boys and they can get married."

Okay. Clearly, I'm getting way ahead of myself. But I always had a dream, a fairy tale of sorts, where my children would marry the children of my friends. Once kids got hitched, the parents were locked together for eternity too. The Gallos were perfect, but they got stuck with my parents. They are not a gift in anyone's life.

"Um, yeah, maybe." He shrugged. "Let us get pregnant first before we start planning a ceremony, okay?"

"Okay." I couldn't wipe the smile off my face. When I'd pushed Frisco and Georgia toward each other, I knew they'd be perfect together. I knew it in my core, even though it took a lot of convincing and underhanded actions on my part. It was worth it because now they're going to have a baby.

"City seemed a little preoccupied when he left this morning. Did he see something last night?"

"Um," I mumbled and twisted my hands in my lap. "No."

"Everything okay?" He looked over at me and frowned.

"We're perfect."

"Then why are you fidgeting all of a sudden?"

My hands stopped moving. "I didn't notice I was. Sorry."

He didn't push again, and I stared out the window and thought about my husband. I didn't think it was *that* big of a deal. Men get it done all the time.

I looked over at him and pulled at my lip. "Let me ask you this, Frisco. 'Cause you're a man."

"Last time I checked, I was." He laughed softly.

"Men," I muttered under my breath. "What's the big deal about vasectomies?"

His head jerked backward and his eyes met mine. "As in, a knife near my balls vasectomy?"

I nodded and shrugged at the same time and probably looked like a moron. "I think that's the only kind."

"I think I answered it."

"How?" I asked, confused.

His hands tightened around the steering wheel, and he kept his eyes pinned to the road. "I just said it… It's a knife near a man's most private area."

"You mean, favorite area." I rolled my eyes. Was every man a pussy?

"Same thing."

"So what? Women go through worse than that in childbirth. It takes five minutes to get the procedure done, and they use like two stitches to close the incision."

He trembled. "The fact that you need a stitch says the cut is way too big."

"Oh, for Jesus's sake. When I had my episiotomy when Gigi was born, I don't even know how many stitches they used to sew me shut."

His eyebrows squished together, almost meeting the wrinkle in his nose. "What the fuck is that?"

"Sometimes, the baby doesn't have enough room to come out. So they have to—"

"Stop!"

My head tipped to the side as I stared at him. "I didn't get to the grossest part."

"You said enough."

"Well, it makes a vasectomy look like a splinter."

"I've never had a splinter on my junk, so I wouldn't know."

"You're all babies."

"I can take a punch to the face, a knife to the gut, hell, even a gunshot...but don't even think about cutting open my stuff."

I rolled my eyes and exhaled. He was just like the rest of them. Even my manly husband would need some convincing. I'd always thought of him as a superhero, but every single one of them had a weakness. His wasn't kryptonite. Nope, it was a knife near his "junk," as Frisco said.

I'd just have to find a way to make it worth his while. If that didn't work, I'd scare the heck out of him and make him run to the nearest doctor's office. Either way...it was going to happen.

CHAPTER 21
SEEING RED
JOE

"ARE we good to go for the Fourth?" I asked Thomas over the phone on my way home from work.

Suzy wanted a party, and she started planning early, before I got the go-ahead from the security team. Sometimes she did that…got ahead of herself.

"Yeah. Everyone is coming—even Tank, Bear, and a few others. We should be covered. If someone tries something there, they'd be a fucking moron and dead to boot."

"Good. She already bought an ass-load of decorations. I would have hated to tell her we had to cancel everything. Any leads yet?"

"I heard it was Rooster and Cowboy who were released on technicalities."

"And they are?"

"Two people that I never wanted to see the light of day. Fuck."

I grimaced as a knot formed in my stomach. "Text everyone their photos."

"On it."

"I'm pulling in. I'll catch you later."

"Did Suzy really ask you for a vasectomy, man?"

I pinched the bridge of my nose. Information moved fast in the Gallo family. "Yeah," I mumbled.

"Do it," he replied sternly.

"What?"

"I did it last year. It's no big deal. It's like a paper cut."

"On my balls."

"Don't be a pussy, Joe. It'll make your woman happy."

"I'll think about it."

"Do you want more kids?" he asked.

My head lurched back at the thought of more children running around the house. "Fuck no. Three girls are enough for me. I'll be in a grave early because of them as it is."

"Then get it taken care of."

"Yes, sir."

"Fuck off."

"Love you," I told him as I disconnected the Bluetooth and ended our conversation.

"So did you think about it?" Suzy asked as she scrubbed my back with her shower scrunchie.

My head hung down and I stared at the bubbles washing down the drain. "I did."

Her hand stilled between my shoulder blades. "Will you do it for me?"

"I'll think about it, sugar." I figured I could buy myself some time before I'd have to go under the knife. I'd do it for her. I'd do anything for her, but I needed time to process this decision.

"Do you want more babies?"

"Do you?"

"No. I don't think I could go through another birth or another round of postpartum depression. I'm happy right now. We have three beautiful girls, and I couldn't imagine another."

"They are pretty amazing, aren't they?"

"They are." She sighed and started to move the strawberry-scented shower gel around my back.

"You know there's no going back once I get it done."

She ducked under my arm and stood in front of me. "I won't change my mind. I don't want another baby, Joe."

Reaching up, I grabbed the sponge from her hand and kissed her lips. The water splashed over us. "I'll give you an answer soon," I whispered.

She wrapped her arms around my neck, pressing

her tits against my chest. Her hand slid down my torso and she fisted my cock. "You like that, baby?" she asked in a sultry voice.

My eyes closed. "I do."

"Then get a freakin' vasectomy if you ever want to feel it inside my body again."

My eyes snapped open, and she dropped my shaft like it was on fire and walked out of the shower. She left me standing there, hard and wet, with no relief in sight. "Suzy, come on," I said, climbing out after her, leaving the water running.

She wrapped the towel around her body. "Nope. This body is no longer yours until you take care of our problem." Her eyes dipped to my cock, which was waving at her or shaking from fear. "Then you're allowed back inside *your sweet pussy*." She said it in the same tone of voice I used when I was inside of her.

My mouth dropped open and I stood there frozen as I watched her walk out of the bathroom, dripping wet.

"Fuck me," I muttered after I realized I hadn't imagined her mimicking me.

I grumbled to myself while I dried off, but I didn't dare argue. I was now officially being punished for wanting an extension.

"Ro's up. She needs to be fed!" she yelled from the bedroom. "Probably needs a new diaper too."

It was going to be a rough couple of weeks until I

finally caved. It would happen. Suzy would make sure of it. I grabbed a pair of shorts off the floor and yanked them on in frustration. "You're an idiot," I told myself as I walked toward the babies' room.

"Hey, Daddy's girl," I said, cradling her in my arms while the bottle warmed up. "Did you have a fun day today?"

She just gurgled and giggled, reaching up and grabbing my nose with her tiny fingers. She had on my favorite onesie—*Kickin' Ass and Takin' Naps* with a skull and baby rattles. Aunt Izzy had bought one for each of the girls. Suzy decided they could wear it in the house but could never be seen in public wearing profanity.

I shook the bottle and took a quick taste to check the temperature out of sheer laziness. I grimaced at the horrid flavor and regretted my decision not to use a patch of skin. Baby formula would never be confused with milk again. It tasted like chalk.

"Yum, right?" I asked as I stuck it in her mouth. Her big, blue eyes widened, and her mouth started to feverishly suck down the contents immediately.

Standing by the patio door, I stared into the backyard, surveying the woods for any movement. The full moon illuminated the tree line, and the wind made the shadows shift across the grass. A red glow about fifty yards away, deep into the woods, caught my eye.

"What is that?" I whispered like Ro would answer me. I squinted, trying to get a better look before the light vanished. I scratched my head with my free hand and wondered if I had imagined it. As I started to turn around, the glow was back and brighter than before. I watched, my eyes glued to the spot, as the light dimmed and brightened repeatedly before vanishing altogether.

When Rose drained her bottle and I placed her against me to burp, I dialed Thomas. "Hey."

"What's up?" he answered with a moan.

"It's probably nothing," I said, feeling uncomfortable because I could tell by the noises that the moan didn't come from a television. "Fuck. Sorry I interrupted."

"You got me now, so spill it."

"I think someone was in the woods."

"I'll be right over," he said before the call dropped, and Ro let out the loudest burp.

For a second, I forgot about the light outside. "That's my girl. Keep burping like that and Daddy won't have to murder any boys until you're in your twenties."

She laughed, grabbing my face with her hands and leaning forward to kiss me but completely missing my lips. Baby kisses were the best. Even though they were messy, they were the purest form of love.

I buried my face in her neck and tickled her with

my whiskers. She squirmed, giggling just like her mother. Whoever was in the backyard would have to kill me before I let them hurt my four girls. Nothing else mattered more than them—not even myself.

"Were you talking to someone?" Suzy asked from behind me, causing me to jump.

"Fuck, you scared me."

"What's wrong?" She walked toward me slowly, pulling her robe tighter around her waist.

"Nothing, sugar. Thomas is coming over."

"Why?" she asked, glancing at the clock. "It's so late."

"He has something he wants to give me." I lied to stop her from panicking. "Why don't you take Ro upstairs, and I'll meet him outside so he doesn't wake the girls."

"Okay. Just be careful." She lifted Ro from my arms and gave me a quick kiss. "I'll meet you upstairs." She smiled over her shoulder before she walked out.

"Oh, yeah? Naked?" I hoped because she'd left me hanging, and at this point, I probably had enough sperm inside me to give her triplets.

"Not on your life." She smiled and turned so I couldn't see her face. "Snip, then sex."

"For the love of—"

"Don't bring Him into it," she yelled down the stairway before my hand could touch the doorknob.

I paced around the front yard and watched the

perimeter of the house as I waited for Thomas. He pulled in just as I was about to start the sweep of the woods myself.

He turned his bike off at the street, letting it glide in whisper-quiet. "Hey. Sorry. Traffic was fucked from an accident."

"It's fine. I was just about to start myself."

He climbed off his sweet new ride—a Night Rod Special. "I'm sure they saw you looking in their direction and took off, but let's check the woods and see if we find something. Show me."

"How's the bike?" I asked as we walked toward the very spot where I'd seen the red dot.

"Fuckin' beautiful, but Angel's a little pissed."

"Why?"

"'Cause she's worried I'm going to wreck."

"She realizes you've been riding all your life, right?"

"Some shit about being a dad and having responsibilities."

"Women."

"Yep."

"How are the balls?"

"Still whole. Over there," I said, pointing to the very spot, off in the distance, and changing the subject.

As we approached, we could see the ground littered with cigarette butts. "Fuck. This is what I was afraid of."

"Someone's watching us." I bent down and picked one up. "Looks like they've been here a while too." The butts were in various stages of decomposition. With the heat, humidity, and rain, it could've been only a few days. Either way, someone had been here and they were waiting for the right time to strike.

CHAPTER 22
SCARE TACTICS
SUZY

"JOE." I slid my arms around his neck as he sat on the couch. Leaning over him, I placed my mouth next to his ear and whispered, "I think I'm pregnant."

He froze and his heart started to pound frantically under my palms. "How?"

"See, when we have sex, your sperm swims up my—"

He tipped his head back and stared up at me. "Woman, I thought you were on the pill."

"I stopped taking it weeks ago."

"Oh, God. Another baby?"

"I'm hoping for another girl," I said, unable to wipe the smile off my face.

I wasn't pregnant. My little talk didn't get him moving on the vasectomy, so I figured radical action needed to be taken.

"I don't think I can take another girl, and the babies are still bottle-feeding."

"Don't worry, baby. They'll be walking by the time our next bundle of joy is born."

He rubbed his forehead with his fingertips as his face drained of color. "I don't know if I can handle this."

"Then why didn't you get snipped?"

He grimaced when his hand fell away. "You know I hate that word."

I grinned, biting the inside of my mouth to stop myself from laughing. My poor husband looked like his worst nightmare just came true. "Sounds better than twins, doesn't it? Now do you wish you had a vasectomy?"

He sighed and nodded slowly. "I do." He swallowed, closing his eyes.

"Good, because I'm not pregnant."

His eyes cut to mine, wide and pissed off. "You're not?"

"Nope." I shook my head and grinned. "Go get it done before you knock me up again."

"Jesus." He gripped his chest and exhaled. "You scared the shit out of me, babe. Not cool."

"So you'll do it?"

"Yeah," he grumbled.

Victory was mine.

"As long as you're sure?"

"I've thought a lot about it, Joe."

"Okay. Are the girls ready to go?" He glanced down at his watch.

"Yeah. Want to help me get them and head over?"

It was Sunday—the first one since we'd been on lockdown with the threat against the entire family.

We climbed the stairs hand in hand, and I couldn't help but think how lucky I truly was. My life was blessed. Somehow, with all the insanity we'd been through, everyone had come out alive. So far. Thinking back on it all, and there was quite a bit, I couldn't believe that we'd survived, that our love had endured, and we'd grown stronger as a couple.

When we walked into the babies' room, Gigi stood between the cribs talking to the girls. We watched at the doorway, peeking through the crack and listening.

"You two gotta be good. Daddy hasn't spanked me, but he does Mommy, and I don't want him to do it to you."

Joe laughed softly, his body shaking against my back. I peered over my shoulder and narrowed my eyes. "We have to talk to her about this," I whispered.

He nodded. "It's kind of cute, though."

"No. It really isn't anymore. She keeps telling everyone how you spank me, Joe."

"Okay, okay. We have time for a quick talk before we head over." Joe reached over me and pushed open the bedroom door. "Hey, baby girl. Whatcha doing?"

Gigi turned to face us wearing her favorite pink

dress that had lace frills around the hemline. She twisted her finger in her hair, twirling it around her knuckle. "Just talking to my sissies."

"What did you tell them?" he asked, walking up to her before scooping her into his arms.

"I told them they have to be good, Daddy." She peered up at him with the sweetest look—the one that usually got her out of trouble. I swear she learned how to bat her eyelashes and get her way from her aunt Izzy.

Joe sat on his knees, cradling Gigi in his arms. "You know I don't spank Mommy because she's bad, right?"

Her eyes widened and her tiny mouth fell open. "You don't?" she whispered.

Joe shook his head and smiled sweetly. "No, baby. It's not that type of spanking."

Her eyebrows drew together. "There's more than one kind?"

"There is."

I glanced toward the ceiling and closed my eyes. There were embarrassing things, and then there were *embarrassing* things. Discussing your sex life with your kid was the worst kind of mortification. She'd probably be scarred for life. Someday, when she was older, she'd have a lot of questions that I still won't want to answer.

"But Billy at school says his dad spanks him when he's bad. So why do you spank Mommy?"

"It's like a kiss," Joe told her, pushing the tiny wisps of hair off her forehead.

"A spanking is like a kiss?" She stared at him and gawked.

Oh, God.

"It's like a love tap. I just touch her butt softly. It's not really a spanking."

She placed her tiny hands on his cheeks and looked into his eyes. "So when you love someone, you touch their butt?"

"Only if you're married."

"I'm so confused," she mumbled.

"Me too, Gigi," I told her and laughed.

"No boy should ever spank you or touch your butt. Understand?" Joe's lips were mushed together by her hands and the words sounded funny.

"Unless I'm married."

"Right, but then, only if you want them to."

"Daddy?" Gigi scooted closer to him, still gripping his face.

"Yeah, baby girl?"

"I don't ever want to get married. I want to live with you and Mommy forever, and I don't ever want to get spanked."

"Your lips to God's ears," I whispered and sighed.

I hated her growing up. She was still little, but every day I could see her changing and growing, becoming her own tiny person. Imagining the day she'd leave home to go to college broke my heart.

"You never have to leave, Gigi. Daddy just wants you to be happy." He pulled her closer, wrapping his arms around her. Her tiny lips found his and she laid a wet one right on him.

"I love you, Daddy."

"Love you too, baby girl. Want to go to Grandma's?"

"Yes!" she screeched and bounced in his lap. "Does that mean Papa spanks Nona?"

"You'd have to ask them, kid."

That will make for an interesting dinner conversation.

CHAPTER 23
GALLO SUNDAYS
JOE

"SUZY GET you to agree to the vasect—" Mike couldn't even get the entire word out without turning white as a ghost.

Poor guy. I knew exactly how he felt.

"Yeah. I told her I would."

"Now Mia's asking me to get one. Suzy started a chain reaction." He bowed his head and rubbed his face. "I don't think I can handle it."

"You made a living from people beating the shit out of you, and a tiny incision is going to scare you?"

His hand slid around to the back of his neck. "It's my balls, dude."

"Did you watch her give birth to Lily?"

"Well, yeah, duh."

"Be happy she didn't come out of your sac."

He shuddered. "Fuck, man. Don't put that image

in my head. Do you know how long it took me not to have nightmares of her birth?"

"For a big man, you sure are a pussy, Mike."

He gripped his chest and smiled. "I'll embrace that shit all day long when it comes to my junk."

"Thomas got it done. He said it's not a big deal."

Mike's mouth fell open and he turned toward Thomas. "You let a doctor cut your nutsack?"

"Man up, Mikey." Thomas didn't even look him in the eye, just kept flipping through the channels of the television.

Mike narrowed his eyes. "You've all been brainwashed by pussy. What about you, Anthony? Are you still fully functional?"

"I have an appointment next week. Max asked right after Suzy. I think they made a pact to get us all under the knife," he grumbled, tapping his foot nervously.

"I knew it." Mike shot up from the couch. "I'm going to tell Mia hell no."

"That should work out well," I mumbled as he stomped off toward the kitchen.

Thomas glanced at me and laughed. "Mia's going to kick his ass."

"Rightfully so," Pop added before returning his attention to his Sunday sports page in the newspaper.

"Get the hell out!" Mia yelled moments later.

"Baby, I won't do it. It's cruel and unusual punishment," Mike told her.

I turned around, waiting for the fireworks to really start and to see if Mike would stand his ground. My money was on Mia.

"You know what's cruel and unusual punishment, Mike?" She poked him in the chest, causing him to stumble backward. "Giving birth to your baby with a giant head and extra-wide shoulders."

"Stop!" he said and closed his eyes. "I don't want to think about it." He waved his hands, trying to block her from poking him again.

"No baby should have a head as large as yours. I almost split in two when Lily was born. That's some cruel and definitely unusual punishment. So get the hell over a tiny cut on your balls. I've had bigger paper cuts that you'll have with a vasectomy."

"Tell my dick that," Mike mumbled, staring down at her finger still pressing into his chest.

"It's your nuts," Anthony yelled from the living room and laughed. "Dumbass."

"Either you get it done or I'll handcuff you to the bed and do it myself." Mia narrowed her eyes at him.

I wouldn't put it past her either. To be with Mike, she had to be a tough cookie.

"I'd listen to the woman," Suzy said, tossing the dishcloth over her shoulder. "She knows how to use a scalpel."

"For shit's sake." Mike looked up to the ceiling and said a little prayer. "Fine."

Mia smiled, finally moving her hand away. "Thank you." She stalked away from him with a satisfied look.

He glanced at me and shrugged. Even the biggest man could lose a battle with a woman. Mike couldn't use his muscles to intimidate her. He thought his balls were his own, but he quickly learned who really wore the pants in the family.

"The Cubs might just do it this year," Pop said, pretending he didn't hear a thing that went on.

"Keep dreamin', Pop," Thomas told him. "Hell hasn't frozen over yet."

"It better happen before I die."

"Who wants dessert? I made cannolis." Mom walked into the living room with an overflowing tray of cannolis and Gigi almost attached to her leg.

"I do," Pop said and set his paper in his lap. After he grabbed one and she started to walk away, he smacked her butt.

"Nana, does Papa spank you because he loves you?" Gigi asked, tugging on Ma's apron.

Ma patted her head with one hand and smiled down at her. "He does, sweetie."

"Daddy's always spanking Mommy too, and she makes this noise..." Gigi started to imitate Suzy's moan, and Ma's smile faded. "It kind of scared me at first, but Daddy said it's because they love each other."

Her eyes darted to mine and I hung my head, unable to look her in the eye. "Gigi, baby—" She paused and chewed on her bottom lip, searching for the right words. "Joe, want to help me out here?"

I cleared my throat. "Um, we already had this talk at home."

Ma narrowed her eyes and sneered before looking to my pop for the rescue. "Sal?"

Suzy sat down next to me and grabbed my hand. "What's everyone looking at each other so strangely for?" she whispered in my ear.

"Gigi asked Ma about spanking."

"Shit." Suzy stood and quickly scurried out of the living room.

"Want to watch *Frozen*?" Pop asked Gigi.

"*Frozen*!" she cheered, her brown hair bouncing up and down as she jumped in place.

"*Frozen*!" Lily yelled, running into the room and almost crashing into Ma.

"Nice," Ma muttered to Pop and shook her head.

He slapped his knee and laughed. "Works every time."

"Coward," Ma whispered before setting two napkins on the floor and placing Lily's and Gigi's cannolis on top. "Sit and watch the movie while the adults have a little chat."

I swallowed, pulling at the collar of my shirt. "I want to watch it too."

"Oh, no, you don't. Get your ass to the adult table for a little talk." She smiled sweetly and glanced around the room at everyone. "Everyone I gave birth to in the dining room." When no one moved, she yelled, "Now!"

Just like we were kids again, everyone scurried into the dining room and took their seats.

"You too, Sal," she told him, and we glanced around the table at each other with our mouths hanging open.

"Someone's mad," Anthony whispered and covered his mouth.

"Jesus," Izzy mumbled and started to laugh when we heard Pop grumbling in the living room.

Ma sat down at the head of the table, brushing her hair back from her shoulders. She sat with her hands clasped in front of her, resting on the table, and looked around the table until Pop sat at the opposite end. "We need to talk about the things your kids are overhearing."

"Ma, I don't think—" Mike started to speak, but Ma waved her hand and cut him off.

"I'm really worried that they're hearing some things that aren't meant for little ears."

Thomas pointed toward me, throwing me under the bus. "That's Joe's fault."

"No." Ma pointed her finger at Thomas and his head jerked back. "I've watched all the babies in this family, and it seems as soon as they can talk, they say the most inappropriate things."

"That's just Gigi, Ma," Izzy joined sides with Thomas.

"Not so, my dear, sweet, dirty daughter." Ma smiled at Izzy instead of waving her finger in her face.

I leaned back in my chair, placing my arm on the back of Anthony's chair and sighed. "What are they saying, Ma?"

"I can't go into specifics. I've never been one to use such language."

Izzy rolled her eyes. "You're so full of shit. Where do you think we learned it?"

"Your father and I—" She touched her neck, stroking it with her index finger. "We kept certain things for inside the bedroom. But you kids, you don't hide anything from your children." She had a straight face when she told that bold-faced lie.

We burst into laughter.

"What's so funny?" she asked, peering around the table with her eyebrows drawn together.

"We heard everything, Ma," Thomas told her, the only one with enough balls to make the confession first.

Ma's head jerked backward like she'd been struck. "What did you hear?"

Anthony raised his hand. "My bedroom was closest to yours. I heard *everything*."

"Everything?" she asked with wide eyes.

"Why do you think I slept with the television on?" He crossed his arms over his chest and smirked. "I had to do something to block out all the racket you two were making."

"Well, I——"

Pop laughed, smacking his hand on the table. "Mar, you were never a quiet one."

"I never thought they could hear." She dragged her hand down one side of her face and cringed.

"Oh! Sal! Harder!" Izzy mimicked my mother's voice, and I almost fell off the chair in laughter at my ma's mortified expression.

"Ah! Good times," Pop added and smiled, nodding as if he was replaying their wild sex life in his head.

"Oh, God," she groaned and put her face in her hands. "How didn't I know?"

"We just never brought it up, but we——" Anthony waved his hands around the table "——we talked about it more than once."

"I just can't——" She pushed herself up from the table and started to walk away. "Go back to watching television," she mumbled without looking back.

Pop just smiled and shrugged. "I tried to gag her, but your mother didn't like it."

I cringed at the thought. "Pop, come on!"

He laughed, finding the topic comical.

"Well, I did."

Izzy shook her head and couldn't look him in the

eye. "Thanks for too much information, Pop." She grabbed a cannoli from the tray and stalked off toward the living room, mumbling curse words to herself.

If Gigi wasn't scarred for life, I sure as fuck was.

CHAPTER 24
IT TAKES A VILLAGE

SUZY

FOR YEARS, Mrs. Gallo has been teaching me to cook. No matter how hard she tried and how much I practiced, nothing ever turned out the same way as hers. The night before the party, the girls decided to come over and help cook. Probably because they wanted to make sure everything would be edible for the guests.

The men promised to stay out of our hair and keep themselves busy. Not only did my brothers-in-law show up, but so did Morgan, Sam, and Frisco. They were going to discuss "man things," whatever that meant. We were just happy they were going to stay out of our way while we cooked.

"How's it going with Frisco around here all the time?" Mia asked while stirring together the dressing ingredients for the biggest bowl of macaroni salad I'd ever seen.

"Fine. He helps with the babies sometimes, but he mostly stays outside."

"Yeah, Morgan too. Even at the clinic, he's outside or in the waiting room. He has to be bored to death."

"Right?" I asked as I uncorked another bottle of wine. "Hopefully, this ends soon so everyone can get back to their lives."

"I kind of like it," Izzy announced, grabbing the bottle from my hands.

I nudged her with my hip and took the bottle back. "That's because they aren't with you all day." I filled my glass and handed it back to her. "James just comes home early from work. It's different for you."

"You've met James, right? Nothing about that man is easy."

"It's not a hardship when you have to spend more time with your husband." Max rolled her eyes, pausing for a minute from chopping the cabbage for the homemade coleslaw.

"Um," Izzy mumbled and raised her wineglass toward Max. "It's James. It's always a hardship."

Max's gaze flickered toward Izzy. "You married him, girl."

Izzy's lips pinched together when she crossed her arms in front of her chest and held the glass of wine near her lips. "He's entirely too serious about this whole situation."

"Rebel," I muttered under my breath.

Izzy squeezed her eyes shut. "What's your point?"

"The man did kidnap you and then—" I couldn't finish the statement. I didn't want to either. We all knew what happened to him. After they found him with Izzy, no one ever saw him again.

"I'd never let that happen again. Nothing is going to happen to any of us." Izzy glanced around the room at each of us, her gaze bouncing from person to person.

"Sure. You're right." Angel nodded, giving Izzy a fake smile.

"You know, I'm the only one here who hasn't been attacked by some crazy ass coming after our men," I shook my head and grimaced. "Correction." I swallowed at the memory. "I was never attacked by a crazy girl or for revenge. Derek was just a douche who didn't realize that no meant no and then there was the guy at the Neon Cowboy." My voice trailed off and I shivered.

Izzy tomahawk-chopped a carrot and seemed to enjoy it. "Fuckin' prick should've lost his pecker."

"Angel, Mia, and Izzy are the ones who have already gone through shit for their guys," Max stated before she started to peel the carrots for the slaw.

"So that means we're good. Once a lifetime is enough. It's someone else's turn this time." Izzy took a sip of her wine with shaky hands before she picked up the knife again.

I placed my hand over hers. "Just relax a minute.

We don't need any fingers inside the macaroni salad, Iz."

She nodded and cupped the wine in both hands. "I just can't believe we're going through this shit again. I thought everything was over with."

"I'm sure Thomas, James, and the rest of the guys will get it sorted soon. No one likes living like this," Angel added when she took a seat next to Max at the table. "They work night and day at trying to track them down. Everyone wants it over, especially Thomas, James, and Sam."

"Do they have a plan?" Mia asked before dumping the pasta into the mayonnaise mixture she had finished stirring.

Angel pushed her red hair behind her shoulders and grinned. "They do. They don't share anything with me, but I still hear their conversations."

Max placed the peeler on the table and smiled at Angel. "You mean you eavesdrop."

Angel shrugged. "Same thing."

Everyone laughed.

"So what's their plan?" Mia asked.

"I don't think we'll have another issue with them again."

I swallowed, almost choking, because I knew what that meant. "That's illegal."

Izzy smacked my arm. "You're such a goody-two-shoes. Do you think the people after them would stop to think if something is illegal, or would they just kill anyone without even a thought?"

"I know." My hand stroked my throat as I tried to smooth down whatever had gotten lodged. "I just don't like the sound of it."

"It's them or us, Suzy. I rather it be any one of us who comes out alive."

"Who needs help in here?" James asked when he walked into the kitchen. Every set of eyes turned toward him.

"We're good," Izzy said and waved the knife in his direction.

"Hey, sugar," Joe said, coming up behind me and wrapping his arms around my waist.

I tipped my head back and rested it on his chest. "Hey, baby. You guys done?"

"Yeah." His hold tightened and he nuzzled his face into my neck. "We thought we'd help so everyone can get the kids and give my parents some time to rest."

"Oh, please," Max said and pulled the jar of mayo in front of her. "They're happy with the babies there. Your ma is in her glory."

The front door opened and closed before Thomas, Mike, and Anthony appeared in the kitchen. "Who needs help?" Anthony asked and shoved his phone in his back pocket. "Kids are good. I just texted Ma."

"See?" Max smiled and jutted her chin out.

"What still needs to be done?" Thomas asked after he gave Angel a kiss.

"What did you guys decide?" Mia asked Mike after she wiped her mayo-covered hands on her apron.

"Nothing to worry your pretty little head about, babe." Mike touched her cheek and cradled her face in his hands.

She punched him straight in the gut, but he didn't even flinch. "Don't treat me like I'm a little girl." He kissed her lips, but she didn't close her eyes or kiss him back.

Mike just shook his head and sighed. "We talked about how to handle security at the party tomorrow. That's all, Mia. Everyone will be in one spot, and so we need to keep everybody safe."

"We could move the party inside," I offered because I hadn't thought about how vulnerable it would make us to even have the party.

"No. We're having the party. We have it covered." Joe turned me in his arms. "No one wants us to change our lives because someone might be after one of us."

I stared up into his beautiful baby blues. "But there's no better reason, babe. Plus, we already changed our lives. I do have Frisco following me around all the time. Remember?"

"I do." His fingers rested under my chin before he

leaned forward. "I don't like another man around you all the time. It's my job to protect you."

"I can protect myself." I grinned.

"Not funny, Suzy."

I pouted and rolled my eyes. "Well, why did you teach me to shoot if you don't want me to use it?"

"It's for when I can't be here, princess."

"Frisco," I added and stood on my tiptoes, pretending I was going to kiss his lips. "He's with me when you're not."

"Don't get used to him being here. Soon this will be over, and he'll be gone."

"I kind of like having him around all day," I teased, which earned me a pinch on the ass. I yelped, reaching back to smooth the spot. "You're the only man I want here all the time."

"You two are making me ill," Izzy said from across the room, throwing a piece of celery that hit me in the cheek.

I glared at her, picking the celery piece from my hair and throwing it back at her. "Says the girl who wears a leash."

"Fuck," Joe muttered and rubbed his face.

"You're just jealous." Izzy stuck her tongue out at me and laughed.

"I kind of am."

"You're all dirty whores," Max added and wiped her hands on a towel. "Coleslaw is done."

"Macaroni salad too." Mia rolled out the tinfoil

and placed it over the bowl before setting it in the fridge. "I think everything is done, actually."

I couldn't help but stare at them all. My family. Years ago, before I met Joe, I'd felt so lonely. I had a sister and parents, but I'd never been as close to them as I was to the people in this room. I never would've imagined I could have this in my life.

"Come on, baby. You can blow me on the way to get the kid," Mike said, untying Mia's apron before tossing it on the counter.

She peered up at him. "Why don't you eat me and I'll drive?"

He rubbed his chin and thought about it for a second. "Impossible."

Mia's eyes flicked upward. "Clearly, God is a man."

Mike leaned forward and invaded her personal space. "I'll make it worth your while when we get home." Mike's eyebrow rose.

Mia crossed her arms in front of her chest. "I want two."

"Two? Isn't that a bit greedy?"

Mia tapped her foot and glared at him.

"All right. All right. Two it is."

"Good," she said and pulled him by the shirt. "Let's go, big boy. You're going to have a busy night."

"Two what?" Angel asked after the front door closed without even a good-bye.

I shrugged. "Whatever it is, I think I want two too."

"Everyone out," Joe said, waving his hands.

"Now?" Anthony asked and looked around the room.

"My woman wants two, and I plan to give them to her."

"Two what?" I asked and turned to face him.

"Anything you want, sugar."

"Hmm," I rubbed my chin and thought carefully about my answer.

"We're out." James slapped Joe on the shoulder before smacking Izzy's ass. "If you're a good girl, I'll let you blow me too."

"Oh, fuck you. You're not the boss of me, ol' man." Izzy laughed and walked toward the door quicker than usual.

"Want to repeat that?" James stalked toward her and picked up the pace.

"You can spank me later." Izzy stopped briefly and wiggled her ass.

"Why couldn't she be born a man?" Joe's mouth turned downward.

I wrapped my arms around his waist. "The world couldn't handle another male Gallo."

"See you tomorrow," Angel said as she walked past us.

"We're out." Thomas followed behind her, taking a second to wave at us before heading for the door.

"Have fun, you two," Max said before the door closed.

We were alone. The girls were asleep. Most of the food was done for tomorrow, and the night was still young. "What do you want to do now?" I asked, burying my face in his shirt and moving my hands down to cover his ass.

He scooped me into his arms, and my legs wrapped around his waist. I yelped when the cold of the wooden table touched my butt. "I have a few ideas," he said against my lips.

His hands slid up my thighs and under my dress. "I do love that you never seem to wear panties anymore."

I nipped his lip, grabbing his bottom one between my teeth before soothing it with my tongue. "I was hoping the night would end like this." My face heated, but it wasn't from embarrassment.

Joe's hands slid the tiny straps of my sundress down my shoulder, letting them rest around my elbows and exposing my breasts. His eyes sparkled and he licked his lips before leaning forward and taking one in his mouth.

My head fell backward, the sensation so strong that my eyes rolled back too. The grip I had on his biceps kept me upright while he moved between my breasts, taking his time with each one.

"Joe," I moaned and wanted more. Needed it more than air.

His hands rested on my back. "Lie back," he whispered against my nipple, sending an entirely different sensation through my body.

Using his hands, he helped lower my back to the table before getting on his knees. "I knew I liked this table for a reason."

His hands looped around my legs and he dragged me forward. Before I could say anything, he put my knees on his shoulders and touched me with his mouth.

Anything that I was about to say vanished. The only thing I could think about was the feel of his tongue on me. Slowly, he kissed my flesh, teasing me without touching the spot I craved.

My fingers tangled in his dark locks and I pulled him closer, smashing myself against his face. "Just a little to the—"

Before I finished my sentence, he covered me with his mouth and shut me up with a simple flick. My entire body lurched forward and moved toward him. "Greedy pussy," he muttered and I almost swallowed my tongue.

Intercourse was amazing, but there was nothing better than the feel of his mouth on me. The way he made love to my body, surrounded me with his warmth. I could lie here all night and let him worship my body this way.

His fingers stroked my opening while he sucked on

my clit. Just when I thought it couldn't get any better, he pushed two inside and I almost came.

As they glided in and out through my wetness, my legs tightened and my knees pressed against the sides of his head. I didn't want him to move or for the feeling to end. He didn't protest, but he became more determined. Licking the spot in the way I liked it most.

Within minutes, sweat covered my body and my fingernails dug into the tabletop so hard it became painful. My ankles locked, pulling him in farther and probably suffocating him in the process.

My back arched, my breathing hitched, and I saw stars. When my body ultimately flattened and I sucked in air as if I were the one being suffocated, my legs finally released their hold on him. He backed away, licking his lips with a very satisfied smile.

"So…" I gasped for air. "…good."

"I'm not done yet, sugar," he said, grabbing my body and flipping me onto my belly.

I was too weak to protest. Too spent from coming to even care.

The familiar sound of a zipper opening filled the room. "Let's go for number two." He pushed inside of me just as my hands found the other side of the table, holding on to brace myself.

"I love your cock," I said without hesitation. Even though I still didn't swear too much in everyday life, I always did when we had sex. He liked it, and if I were being honest with myself, I did too.

"You want my cock inside of you?" He thrust deeper, grunting as he did.

"Deeper. Fuck me harder." I smiled, catching our reflection in the window. His hand wrapped around my ponytail, pulling me against him as he pummeled me. "Just like that. More."

His right hand gripped my hip, his fingers digging into my skin so roughly I'd probably bruise. I bit my lip, trying to stop myself from crying out from the pleasure. Because if Gigi woke up right now, neither of us would be happy.

I couldn't take my eyes off the window. Watching him as he fucked me had to be, hands down, one of the sexiest things I'd ever seen. Seeing other people was a secret thrill I realized after being at the club, but being in on the act and watching it took it to another level.

Feeling the familiar build inside me, I stood on my tiptoes and pushed back, meeting him thrust for thrust. He grunted, releasing my hair and resting his hand on my shoulder. He held me against him as his body bumped into mine, driving his cock deeper inside of me.

My body tightened and I couldn't hold out, letting myself spiral straight into orgasm number two. My mouth fell open, but no air entered my lungs as I watched him, transfixed as he followed me into bliss before collapsing onto my back.

"Daddy," Gigi said from behind us. "Where's Mommy?"

I almost died of embarrassment.

Joe stilled. "Go back to bed, Gig. Mommy will be there in a minute."

She'd probably be scarred for life.

"Fuck," I whispered.

"I can see Mommy's feet. Is she okay?"

I peered around Joe and saw Gigi in her *Frozen* pajamas holding her favorite teddy bear and rubbing her eyes. "I'll be right there, baby. Go upstairs. Daddy was just helping me." I swallowed, panicking and dying a bit inside.

"I was helping your mom get the knot out of her hair."

"Oh, okay," she mumbled before turning around and heading toward the stairs.

My face met the table harder than I had planned. "Damn it." I wanted to hide and never have to discuss this moment ever again. "What a nightmare."

"It's no big deal, sugar."

"You can go to the school and explain it when she tells her teacher about what she saw."

Joe laughed before pulling out of me. "I'm sure the teacher will understand. Shit happens."

"Well, the principal already thinks we're

depraved." I pushed myself off the table and adjusted my dress.

"She needs to get fucked."

"Probably, but it doesn't make it any easier." I blew out a breath and glanced at the ceiling before heading toward Gigi, hopefully, not to explain what she just witnessed.

He grabbed my arm and pulled me back against his chest. "I'll handle the principal. You handle the kid."

"Pussy," I whispered when I collided with his chest, and I didn't feel a bit dirty using the colorful language.

He laughed and rubbed his semi-erect dick against my belly. "Keep talking like that and we're going for three."

"That's the last taste you're getting until you get snipped." I touched his face, running my fingers down his stubble.

"Why do you have to refer to it as snipped?"

"Just get it done."

His eyebrows drew together. "Can't we talk about it?"

"We just did." I kissed his chin and left him standing there with his mouth hanging open.

CHAPTER 25
SHITSHOW

JOE

"HEY, JOE." Sam stood at my side with his lovely wife, Fiona. "Do you need any help with that?" He pointed toward the grill as I turned the hot dogs.

"You think you're man enough?"

He turned to face me and I could feel his glare. "Ever going to stop being a prick?"

I shrugged and turned over the last one. "Probably not."

"You're an asshole."

"I know, but so are you. Embrace it."

"Come on, Fi, let's go where we are wanted."

"Sam," I grunted because suddenly I grew a conscience. "Stay. We gotta talk."

"I think I'll just go talk to Izzy for a bit," Fiona told him and gave me a shitty look.

"No, stay, Fiona. Please." I glanced at her and gave her an I've been an asshole smile. "I'm sorry,

Sam. I know you're not the same person you were before."

He crossed his arms in front of his chest and widened his stance. "I'm not, but clearly you're just as big of a dickhead as you've always been."

"I'm trying to apologize. You've been good to my family. Hell, you've been around long enough you're like an adopted member. I promise to be nicer and treat you as an equal. You just have to understand, we all give each other shit. I can't be too nice or it wouldn't be right. Ya know what I mean?"

His eyes flickered to the ground and then to Fiona before returning to me. "So you want to put everything in the past?" He cocked his head and narrowed his eyes.

I nodded and held my hand out to him. "Can we start over?"

His hand slid into mine. "It's water under the bridge, City. I let it go long ago. You were the one still with the problem."

"It wasn't fair of me. I'm sorry to you, Fiona. Sam's a good man. I couldn't be happier that you two found each other." I didn't add the bit that I was happy he wasn't banging my sister anymore.

Her arm snaked around his back before resting her head against his arm. "Sam really looks up to you like a big brother, Joe. He thinks of you as family."

I grimaced. "I'm sorry to both of you for always being an asshole. Sam and I have a past. We've been through a lot of shit together, but when push comes to shove, he's always been there for me. It's about time I step up to the plate and do the same."

"That means a lot, man."

"Joe!" Suzy yelled from the patio and waved her arms frantically.

"I gotta run. Here—" I handed the tongs to him. "You're on dog duty now. Welcome to the family."

I jogged toward her, worried that something was wrong. "What's up, sugar?"

"There's a phone call for you."

"Who is it?" I asked, taking the phone from her hand.

"I don't know. They wouldn't give a name."

My muscles tensed. "Hello," I said through clenched teeth.

"We're watching," the raspy voice on the other end said before hanging up.

Suzy grabbed my arm. "What did they say?"

"Nothing. Wrong number." I lied through my teeth and scanned the yard for Thomas. "Is the food almost done?" I asked and changed the subject.

She kept trying to make eye contact, but I couldn't look her in the eyes. "Yeah. Just have to take the last few things out of the fridge. How about the stuff on the grill?"

"It's ready when you are. Take everything out, and I'll get everyone to start making their way toward the house."

"Are you sure everything is okay?"

"I'm sure." I kissed her on the forehead and quickly headed toward James and Thomas, who were huddled near the pool, discussing something.

"What's wrong?" James asked, seeing me approaching with clenched fists.

"Someone just called. Said they were watching and hung up."

Thomas's eyes darted toward the woods. "I'll let the guys know. We all need to be on high alert."

"Should we move the party inside?" I asked, glancing around the yard.

"No. I don't want to freak everyone out. Just watch your back and keep your eyes open for anything weird."

"I don't know about this, man," James said and rubbed the back of his neck. "I have a bad feeling about this."

"That makes two of us," I mumbled, rocking back on my heels.

"Dinner!" Izzy shouted from the patio and banged a giant spoon against an empty metal pot. "Come and get it!"

"We got this." Thomas slapped me on the back, trying to play it cool, but I knew he was just as freaked out by this as I was, plus he had the biggest bull's-eye on his back.

Not me.

"Son, everything okay?" my father asked me

before my feet touched the patio, stopping me in my tracks.

"I don't know, Pop." I pinched the bridge of my nose and stared at the ground. "Only time will tell."

"I brought my gun." He patted his shirt, the bulge clearly visible underneath.

"Let the guys handle it," I told him and moved his hand away from the piece.

"Joe, I may be old, but I can still kick your ass and shoot a straight shot."

"No doubt," I laughed.

CHAPTER 26
FIREWORKS
SUZY

"I'M SO FULL," I moaned, rubbing my stomach while I lay on the pool lounger.

"I never want to eat another hot dog again," Race said from beside me, holding her stomach too.

"I don't know how you eat that shit." Max wrinkled her nose.

"Max, drop the bullshit," Mia told her, plopping into a chair next to Max at the table.

"Did you notice the guys seem more tense since the party started?" Angel poured another glass of lemonade and glanced around the yard, zeroing in on the guys huddled in one area. "See?" She pointed toward them.

"Something's up, but they're being pretty tight-lipped," Izzy said, sitting near my feet with her legs dangling in the water.

"Anyone notice anything?" Angel asked.

"Someone called, but Joe said it was the wrong number."

"Hmm." Izzy rubbed her chin and stared in James's direction. "Something's up and I'm going to figure out what." She pushed herself up to her feet, jutted out her chest, and strutted in his direction.

"She acts like she's the boss, but we all know the truth," Angel said and laughed.

"No matter what, I still think she has James by the balls," Max said before pushing out her chair, creating the worst sound of the metal scraping against the cement.

I cringed. "Must you?"

Max rolled her eyes. "I'm going to check on the kids. Anyone need anything while I'm up?"

"We're good," I said, answering for the group. "Let me know if Ma needs help inside with the kids."

Mrs. G had been inside most of the day, preferring to surround herself with the babies than adults. Fran had joined her too, but she had brought a wine bottle with her before she disappeared inside.

I turned toward Race. "How's Fran been treating you?"

"She's been really good. She's too busy with Johnny to be up in our shit lately, and I'm too busy with the track to care."

I wasn't jealous of her. That wouldn't be the right

word. I envied her. For her independence and not being tied down by a gaggle of children. She owned a business and lived out her dreams.

"I told you Fran just needed a man." I smiled, thinking back to when she blew into town. I thought Mrs. Gallo was involved in her kids' lives, but I learned what it meant to be a helicopter parent the moment I met Fran.

Morgan wanted to start a new life away from Chicago, taking a job with Thomas at ALFA Investigations. He hadn't expected his mother to uproot her life and follow him to Florida. After his stint in the military, she claimed she couldn't live without him anymore.

"Well, Johnny was a game changer. She actually seems happy." Race pulled down her sunglasses, blocking the glare from the setting sun.

I sighed, placing my hand over my eyes to get a better view of our guys and noticed Izzy heading back our way. "We all want love. Doesn't matter how old we are."

The guys stood near the tree line, talking and scanning the yard every few moments. They looked like a small army of tattooed sexiness. Mike, James, Joe, Anthony, Thomas, Sam, Morgan, Frisco, Bear, and Tank huddled together.

"Maybe they're talking about where to set up the fireworks," I told the girls, but I didn't believe a word.

Something was up, but as usual, they weren't sharing with us.

"They stopped talking when they saw me. Something is definitely up." Izzy sat back down, her brown hair flowing down her back as she placed her feet back in the pool.

Georgia walked out of the house. "Hey, girls. Sorry. I was inside spending time with Mrs. Gallo and the kids."

"How are the babies?" I asked, too full to move.

"Having fun with Grandma." Georgia took a sip from her beer before holding the cold mug up to her forehead. "It's hotter than Hades out here."

"Maybe we should take this party inside, girls." Mia dragged her lemonade across the table and pressed it to her neck. "Between the view of our guys and the sun, I'm overheating."

I laughed. I knew exactly what she meant. "Drinks inside?" I pushed myself up from the lounger. "I have champagne chilling in the fridge."

"You better have more than one bottle." Izzy turned to me. "I could down one myself without sharing."

"That's different than any other day, how?" Mia said and shook her head.

I bent down next to Izzy and scooped water in my hands, pouring it over my shoulders before smearing it around my neck. "Let's go inside until the sun goes down and it cools off a bit. We'll come back out before fireworks."

I didn't have to say it twice. Everyone followed me inside, collapsing in the kitchen.

"Why do we live in this hot-ass state, again?" Izzy whined.

"You'd rather make snow angels?" Mia teased her and grabbed the bottles of champagne out of the fridge.

Izzy's lip curled in disgust. "Hell no."

"Just open this and be quiet." Mia shoved the bottle in front of Izzy's face.

"Your hair looks really cute today, Suzy. Did you do something different to it?" Angel asked as she pulled down the champagne glasses from the cabinet next to the fridge.

"That's because Daddy took a knot out of her hair," Gigi said, strolling into the kitchen and overhearing us.

"He did?" Izzy asked and set the bottle down on the table before holding out her arms for Gigi. "Was Daddy doing Mommy's hair?" Izzy set Gigi on her lap and started to tickle her.

Gigi squealed and squirmed in her arms. "Right here, he helped her, Aunt Iz." She pointed at the table.

Izzy peered at me over Gigi's head, and heat crawled up my neck. "Kids." I grimaced, trying to deflect my embarrassment.

"Mommy was moaning and Daddy was grunting, so I think it was a big knot."

I died a little bit inside.

"Oh, it sounds like it was hard." Izzy giggled and winked at me, which earned her a middle finger since Gigi wasn't looking at me.

Gigi put her hands on Izzy's cheeks and brought her face closer. "Does Uncle Jimmy help you with your hair too?" The innocent look on her face made my heart melt.

"He does sometimes, baby girl." Izzy kissed Gigi's nose. If I didn't know better, I'd think Gigi was a clone of Izzy. They were two peas in a pod. Not only did Gigi have the Gallo traits, the two of them had the same spitfire personality.

"Naked? Daddy's butt was hanging out." Gigi wrinkled her nose.

"Sometimes."

Gigi's eyes grew wider and she brought her face closer to Izzy's, smashing her cheeks more. "Why?"

"Because that's what couples do. You'll understand when you're older," Izzy told her and rubbed her back.

"I don't ever want a boyfriend. They're gross, Aunt Iz."

Izzy pulled her closer, cradling Gigi in her arms. "They are, Gigi. Don't ever have a boyfriend."

"Mommy and Daddy boss me around enough, I

don't need a man to boss me around like Uncle Jimmy does you."

I bit my lip to hold in my laughter as my eyes met Izzy's. We often think our kids don't really see what's going on—that they're too young to understand. Even with their innocence, they see everything that happens around them.

"Uncle Jimmy doesn't boss me around." Izzy stroked Gigi's hair and started to rock back and forth in the chair.

Gigi twirled a strand of Izzy's hair, the same shade of brown as her own, around her finger. "Does he spank you? Daddy spanks Mommy when she's bad."

Izzy dragged her eyes to mine. "Sometimes I get a spanking when I'm bad too. Just like when you're a bad girl, Gigi."

"But Mommy seems to like it when Daddy spanks her, Aunt Izzy. When I'm a bad girl, I get a time-out, not a spanking. So why does Mommy get spanked?"

I pinched the bridge of my nose and wished for a quick escape. Not this again.

"You'd have to ask her, Gigi."

"Mommy?" Gigi said, turning her face toward me.

I stood quickly because I couldn't answer her with a straight face, and I didn't want to have to explain my sex life to my child. "I think I hear Joe calling for me. I'm sure Aunt Izzy can explain it to you."

I walked out of the kitchen before anyone could stop me, especially Gigi. I dreaded the day I'd have to explain the birds and the bees. The day she realized Daddy wasn't punishing me for being bad would be the day I'd want to crawl into a hole and hide. Above all, hopefully, she'll realize how much her father and I loved each other.

CHAPTER 27

BANG BANG

JOE

"I'LL SHOOT off the fireworks. The rest of you keep your eyes on the perimeter." Morgan bent down and grabbed the grill lighter.

"You know what you're doing, man?" Frisco asked, dragging his fingers through his hair.

"I was shooting off fireworks when you were still jackin' off to tittie magazines." Morgan smirked before letting out a booming laugh. "I got this."

"Let's spread out." Thomas pointed around the yard where our friends and family sat on their blankets, waiting for the fireworks display to start.

"I have a bad feeling about this." Mike shifted from foot to foot before stalking off to the right corner of the woods.

"It'll be fine," Sam said before jogging off in the opposite direction.

I smoothed my hands down my pants, wiping off

the sweat that had started to coat my palms. For once, I agreed with Mike. I had a shitty feeling. Just days ago, someone had been sitting in the woods, watching me, and now everyone I cared about sat on the lawn in plain view.

"Joe, come with me," Thomas said, yanking on the sleeve of my shirt to get my attention.

"Right," I muttered and looked over my shoulder at Suzy, Gigi, and the babies, spread out on a blanket near the door to the patio. My heart ached at the thought of anything happening to them.

There wasn't one person sitting in the yard that I could handle losing. Even Sam. No one deserved to lose their life to the shitheads from the Sun Devils MC. The government was supposed to protect Thomas's and James's identities, but just like everything else, it could be bought for a price.

When the first firework exploded above, I jumped. "Fuck." My heart started to race and I shook my hands out, rolling my head on my shoulders to let go of some of my anxiety. I caught a glimpse of the red embers as they cascaded toward the ground.

Thomas turned to face me, placing his hands on my shoulders. "Relax, Joe. Nothing will happen to anyone."

"I wish I had your confidence, brother."

"Just breathe. This will all be over soon."

"How do you know?" I don't know if I'd ever

been as fearful as I was in that moment. Not for myself, but for my family.

"They won't stay hidden for long. They can smell the blood."

For fuck's sake—his words didn't bring me solace.

I stood next to Thomas, trying to keep an eye on the woods and not get distracted by the sound of the fireworks. Every time one exploded, my eyes would dart around the yard to make sure it was only the fireworks and nothing else.

The hair on the back of my neck stood at full attention. Movement in the woods caught my eye. "Thomas," I narrowed my eyes, honing on the same familiar red glow in the distance. "Over there."

He turned slowly. "Act normal. Don't give it away that we've spotted him. Walk with me." He motioned with his chin toward the woods in the direction of the glow.

Slowly, we made our way into the woods, pulling our guns out of the back of our pants as we walked. The guy got away last time, but there was no way in hell it would happen again.

Less than a hundred feet into the woods and the light disappeared. Thomas motioned to head to my right while he headed to the left. Hopefully, we'd come up behind him without him knowing we were heading in his direction.

I listened for the sounds of branches breaking

under the feet of whoever was watching us from the woods, but I heard nothing.

All that mattered was making him run in the opposite direction of the family.

My feet moved faster, matching my heartbeat as I pushed aside the twigs. The sound of a breaking branch in the distance made my breathing falter.

I took off running, heading straight toward the noise, seeing Thomas doing the same out of the corner of my eye.

A loud bang rang out, and I thought it was firework until Thomas fell to the ground. *Oh God!* Thomas's body crumpled and I ducked, trying to find out where the shot came from.

Every muscle in my body tightened and the adrenaline kicked in, pushing me forward after the intruder when I heard another branch crack.

I didn't have time to stop.

I needed to get the man who had just shot my brother in order to keep everyone else safe. My hands shook, gripping the gun tighter than I should have as I ran in the direction of the gunshot. Tree branches smacked me in the face, blocking my way as I got closer.

The distance between us shortened, but before I could get to him, another gunshot rang out. I didn't stop running, picking up the pace and heading straight into danger. If it took my life to keep everyone else safe, it was worth it. No one would hurt what was mine. No one could take them away from me. Holding the gun in front of me, I cleared the brush and saw James standing above something on the ground.

"Joe! It's me. Don't shoot," he said, hunching over and resting his hands on his knees with the gun still in one hand. "I got him." He sucked in a breath.

I turned to where Thomas had gone down and saw lights in the distance. "He shot Thomas," I told him, running up to the body and looking down, clutching my chest.

"Fucking Cowboy." James spit on him and he moaned, gurgling up blood as it started to ooze from his mouth. "Piece of shit."

"What the fuck, man? How did you get here so fast?"

"I came around from the back before Morgan started shooting off the fireworks. I just didn't get here quick enough." He straightened and wiped his forehead with the back of his hand, still clutching the gun.

"He's not dead." I pointed toward the piece of shit and stood with my feet wide apart, lifting my gun and pointing it at him.

"He will be." James wrapped his hand around my wrist. "He won't last long. Don't shoot him, man."

My hand shook and my finger started to squeeze the trigger.

"Don't do it, Joe. I know you want to, but you'll go

to jail. Think of your family." He pushed my hand down, slowly removing the gun from my hand.

My arm was still extended with trembling hands. "I should've been the one to shoot him, James."

"Killing someone, no matter whom, is a guilt you don't want on your conscience."

We both stood over him as he reached into the air like we were going to help him. We stared down at him, watching him gasping for breath before his hand fell to the ground and he grew silent.

"He's not my first kill, Joe," James admitted and shook his head. "I know how to deal with it."

What do you say to someone when they admit they've killed people? Fuck if I know. "Thomas," I whispered, turning my back on the bastard who had shot my brother.

James and I took off, running toward the lights in the distance. "The ambulance is on the way!" Pop yelled before we were even within fifty feet of Thomas.

Angel sat at his side, clutching his shirt and crying into his chest. "Thomas!" she yelled through her tears, gasping for air out of fear.

"Fuck," I said, feeling tears threatening to fall. "This shouldn't have happened."

Izzy ran to James, wrapping herself around him in tears. "Is he going to die, James?"

"I don't know, baby. Let me look at him." James

untangled her, handing her off to me before kneeling down next to Thomas.

His eyes fluttered open. "Angel," he whispered, reaching up and touching her face.

"Thomas!" she yelled, leaning over him and kissing his face. "Thomas, are you okay, baby?"

"I don't know." He grimaced and closed his eyes again.

"Someone give me a light," James said, holding his arm in the air.

Izzy pressed a few buttons on her phone and turned on the flashlight before handing it to her husband. "It's a pretty big hole. We gotta get him to the house."

The sound of the ambulance going down the street that ran between the house and woods broke through the sobs and panic.

"I'll carry him," James said, scooping his arms underneath Thomas.

"I can do it," I said, pushing him out of the way. He was my brother, and he took a bullet instead of me. When I lifted him, my legs started to shake, but I didn't let it stop me.

I walked quickly, trying to avoid hitting any branches on my way to the yard. When we emerged, the entire family stood around, holding their hands over their mouths in tears.

"Joe," Suzy screeched and ran toward me with her arms outstretched. "Oh my God, Thomas."

"I have to get him to the front yard." My voice was strangled, and he had started to feel like a ton of bricks in my arms.

"Thomas!" Ma yelled from across the yard, running in our direction.

I didn't stop and let her see him. It was too important to get him to the front yard when the paramedics arrived. When I rounded the house, the ambulance pulled into the driveway. Two men hopped out and started running toward us with their gear.

I collapsed onto the ground, shielding Thomas from the impact. Laying him down, I scooted away on my ass and made room for the paramedics.

The enormity of the situation hit me when Suzy wrapped her arms around me from behind and whispered, "He's going to be okay, Joe."

I lost it.

Tears streamed down my face and my entire body started to shake. I grabbed her hands, clutching them to my chest as I watched them work on my brother.

"He's critical," the one man said as they lifted him onto the gurney.

"Oh, God," I said, staring up at the stars before sealing my eyes shut and saying a prayer. Thomas didn't deserve to go out like this.

"Mrs. Gallo," the nurse said, walking into the waiting room. She was met with five women who said yes. "Mrs. Thomas Gallo."

"Yes," Angel said, pushing the others to the side.

"They've taken your husband into surgery to try to control the internal bleeding and remove the bullet."

Angel grabbed her chest, twisting her shirt in her fist. "Will he live?"

"It's too soon to say, ma'am, but the doctors are doing everything they can."

Her legs started to give way, and Suzy grabbed her around the waist, catching her before she collapsed to the floor.

"He's strong, Angel. He'll make it," Suzy whispered to her and stroked her hair.

Angel sobbed, walking backward toward the waiting room chairs with Suzy's assistance. "I can't lose him."

"I knew something bad was going to happen," Mike said, smashing his head into the wall behind us.

"We all made the decision, Mike." I stood, needing a bit of space. I couldn't believe we were here again. Too much time had been spent in hospitals.

Ma was around the corner, leaning against the wall for support.

"Ma," I whispered and pulled her into my arms.

"No mother should outlive her children, Joseph,"

she cried, burying her face in my chest and fisting my T-shirt in her hands.

I held her head in my hands. "Shh, Ma. He'll make it." I promised her something I knew I couldn't deliver.

"You don't know that," she whispered, peering up into my eyes as tears streamed down her face.

If we lost Thomas because of tonight, I didn't know how I'd hold it together. Without him, we might just fall apart.

CHAPTER 28
SAYING GOOD-BYE

JOE

"I CAN'T GO IN THERE." I pointed toward the church.

"Come on, baby. We have to." Suzy grabbed my hand and squeezed.

I shook my head and stared at the ground. "I just can't, Suzy. That's my brother in there."

"Joe." She straightened my tie and peered up at me. "You're strong. You can do this. Just breathe. Everyone is waiting for us."

I rested my head on hers and tried to control my breathing. "How am I supposed to look at him in a —" I couldn't even say the word.

"We have to do this. Do it for him and for your family."

I still hadn't gotten over the trauma of the entire experience. I was always the strong one. The one who never crumpled under pressure, but watching my brother take a bullet had changed me.

I wiped my face and shook out my hands before I pulled on the collar of my suit. "I can't breathe in this fucking thing."

She popped open the top button and loosened my tie. "Better?" she asked, giving me a sorrowful smile.

I pressed my lips to her forehead and let her smell and feel calm me. I couldn't walk in the door of the church without her. "Yeah."

"Come on, baby." She wrapped her arms around my back and ushered me toward the doors to the church.

I walked slowly, unable to take my eyes off Thomas's lifeless body. His pale face devoid of emotion and lying motionless in the casket made my heart seize and beat out of rhythm.

I wanted to wrap my hands around the neck of the bastard that did this to our entire family and watch them gasp for their last breath, begging for mercy they wouldn't receive.

My mother wept in the front pew, dabbing her eyes and staring straight at her son. "I just can't," she whispered as I sat down next to her. My father held her hand so tightly that both of their fingers had turned white.

I put one arm around Suzy's shoulders and the other around my mother's. This was the same church where Suzy and I were married and each of my siblings had said their vows. So many happy memories in a place filled with so much sorrow. I held them tighter, bringing them closer to me as I stared at Thomas, unable to take my eyes off of him.

The priest walked out and made the sign of the cross before beginning to speak. I tuned out, unable to listen. I sat in silence, holding my ladies and thinking about all the stupid shit I'd done in my life that could've put me in the casket instead.

I wasted so much of my youth acting like a fool, feeling invincible, without a care in the world. How quickly my life could've ended never entered my mind. I certainly didn't think about how it would've affected my family.

Suzy settled me down.

She grounded me.

I never had anything to lose until I had her and my girls.

I glanced over at Angel, sitting on the other side of my father. She was frozen, her eyes glued to her husband. Silent tears streamed down her face, stopping near her open lips before falling off her chin.

The mass was a blur. I didn't hear anything the priest said or James's speech about Thomas. None of it mattered.

When everyone in the pews stood, I did too. When they knelt, so did I. I followed their motions like a robot lacking all emotion. There was something mechanical about the motions. I'd shed too many tears in the last week—so much sorrow that my heart couldn't bear another moment without bursting.

When everyone started to murmur and file out of the church, our row finally stood and followed. There were no words that could be spoken, no more emotions left to give.

I hung back with Sam, James, Mike, Anthony, Bear, Morgan, Frisco, and Tank to carry the casket and place him in the hearse to head to the cemetery.

When the front doors closed and the church was empty, we all breathed a sigh of relief.

"Do you think they fucking bought it?" James asked, peering down at Thomas.

His eyes opened and he grimaced when he sat up. "I hope so." He climbed out, holding on to the edge because he was still weak and sore from the surgery. "I had a cockroach crawling on me for the last thirty minutes. I don't ever want to go through that shit again."

"You're a tool," Mike muttered and punched him in the arm.

"Why does everyone look so damn sad?" Thomas stretched and cracked his neck. "It's not like your asses were pretending to be dead."

Even though it was a ruse, it still sucked. Seeing my brother lying there, even if he was alive, was harder than I thought possible.

"Even though you were pretending, it didn't make

it any easier, ass wipe." Anthony closed the lid to the casket and started to buckle the locks.

"All that matters is that the leftover assholes from the MC think I'm dead."

"I think Ma's cries and Angel's weeping were enough to sell it to any jury."

"Good." Thomas laid his hand on top of the coffin. "I'm happy you're not burying me today. I'm not done raising a little hell yet."

"I plan to grow old with you, brother," I told him and nudged him in the shoulder.

"Now, go before anyone gets suspicious. I'll hang with Father O'Toole until tonight and head back to the house when we know the coast is clear."

"You have to lay low for at least a week, Thomas. The guys and I will handle work. You just recover."

"I plan to do nothing but stay in bed. Scout's honor." He made the sign of the cross over his heart, but we all knew he was full of shit.

"Let's go." I grabbed the handle, waiting for everyone else to do the same. We lifted it in unison and carried it to the doorway, leaving Thomas behind us.

I glanced over my shoulder as he disappeared behind the altar. When the doors swung open and we saw the rear of the hearse open and waiting, we all pretended that the coffin was heavier and that my brother was still inside. After we set it down and the mortician moved it inside, we headed toward our cars and our waiting family.

"I think the coast is clear," James said, sliding in next to me.

"That was so hard," Ma said, dabbing her cheeks. "I don't know if I can do that again at the cemetery."

"You can do it, Mar." Pop held her close and kissed her temple. "It's almost over."

"Seeing Thomas in that casket, even knowing that he wasn't dead, almost broke me, Sal."

"I know, baby, but he's okay. We're all okay." Pop looked at me, giving me a sheepish smile.

Suzy curled into my side and placed her hand over my heart. "Life isn't boring in this family. I'm just happy everyone is okay." She smiled up at me and I smiled back.

"I know, sugar. I love you," I told her, covering her hand with mine.

"I love you too, Joe." She rested her head on my shoulder and closed her eyes.

I couldn't help but think about how close we'd come to this being a real funeral. I realized how much I liked boring. I wanted it. The adrenaline rush of people chasing me had worn off.

I was ready for it all to disappear.

Maybe now that the members of the Sun Devils MC thought Thomas was dead and another member of their crew was gone, we could live in peace.

CHAPTER 29
WHAT'S NORMAL?

SUZY

"SO IT'S OVER?" I asked Joe after shaking the last guest's hand as they walked out of Angel and Thomas's house.

We had to do everything as if Thomas had really passed. After the burial, all of the members of the family were invited back to Angel's home for a meal. I never understood why, though. Why did the grieving family have to feed everyone for coming to say good-bye?

"It is." He kissed the top of my head. "Thomas said based on intel and the death of Cowboy, we're in the clear."

"For now," I mumbled and buried my face in his shirt.

"Forever." He stroked my hair softly, soothing me.

"We're Gallos. Trouble seems to find us." I smiled into his chest.

"Look who's alive," James said when Thomas walked through the back door.

"You'd miss me if I wasn't here, buddy."

"I would, asshole." James smiled at him.

"Who wants a beer? I could fucking use one after a day like today." Thomas headed toward the kitchen and whistled.

"I think I'm going to be sick." Angel covered her mouth and ran from the room.

My heart ached for her. Even though it was a lie, I couldn't imagine seeing Joe in a coffin.

"I'm going to go check on her, baby." I touched his cheek, running my fingers against the tiny stubble that had started to form.

"I'll be here waiting. We can leave when you're ready."

"Let's stay a while. I think everyone needs some family time." I patted him on the chest, holding his hand as I walked away until distance separated us.

"Angel," I whispered and pushed open her bedroom door to find her in a ball on the bed. "Oh, sweetie." Lying down next to her, I pushed her hair away from her face. "Everything is okay, sweetheart."

"I couldn't breathe all day, Suz." She turned on her back and stretched out. "I just kept picturing him in that casket for real. I don't know what I'd do without him." Her eyes roamed around the ceiling and she started to hyperventilate.

I grabbed her hand, squeezing it. "He's fine, Angel. Relax."

"I was so close to losing him. More than once, we've almost been torn apart. My heart couldn't survive without him." Tears started to trickle down her cheeks, plopping onto the bedspread.

"I can't imagine losing Joe either. Somehow, other people survive when they lose the love of their life."

"I'd die of a broken heart," she whispered, wiping her face with the back of her fingers.

"We'd help you through it. We're all going to be there sometime." I frowned. I'd probably die of a broken heart too. Joe was more than just my husband —he was my everything. "We'd make it through it for our kids." I turned on my back and stared up at the ceiling, watching the fan as it turned.

"Angel," Thomas said from the doorway. "Are you okay, baby?"

"I'll let you two talk," I said, scooting off the bed.

Thomas smiled as I walked past him and whispered, "Thanks."

"We're doing shots, Suzy Q. Want one?" Izzy held up the bottle of tequila and smirked.

My stomach turned at the thought of getting wasted, especially on tequila. "No, I'm good."

"You're never any fun." She poured another round before pushing them across the counter to everyone else.

"I have infants to take care of when I get home," I told her, feeling like a party pooper.

"I'll give you a pass this once."

I'd probably had fifty passes over the years.

"Let's do a toast." Anthony held his shot glass in the air and waited. I grabbed a bottle of water and joined everyone with my bottle high above my head. "To the Gallos, one kick-ass family that even a gunshot doesn't stop."

Mia cleared her throat and grinned. "Gunshots, punches, and everything else, but don't mention a vasectomy without them scurrying away like little rats." She raised her glass higher.

"Salute," everyone murmured, not willing to make a comment after that.

"What a bullshit day," Anthony said, pulling a stool up to the counter and making himself comfortable.

Max stood behind him with her arms wrapped around his neck. "I kept waiting for Thomas to move and hear someone in the church scream." She laughed, nuzzling her face into his neck.

"That would've been kick-ass," Anthony said, turning his face to kiss her forehead.

Izzy leaned on the counter and wound her fingers with James's. "Don't ever make me go through that."

He grinned. "I have it in my will that you're to be buried with me like the slaves in Egypt. You're coming to the afterlife with me, baby."

She punched him in the gut and he hunched over. "Bull-fuckin'-shit."

He laughed and held his stomach. "I thought you'd love the idea."

I giggled and glanced over at Joe, who was digging his fingers into his eyes.

"Where did Ma and Pop go?" Thomas asked as he walked back into the kitchen with Angel under his arm.

"They were exhausted and headed home," Izzy told him and picked up the bottle of tequila again. "Shot?"

"I think I'll stay sober tonight."

Izzy's mouth fell open and she gawked at Thomas. "Why?"

"Just fuckin' with ya. Pour me a shot." He laughed and nudged Izzy in the shoulder.

"Christ, you scared me."

There was a low hum in the kitchen as everyone stood around chatting like it was normal. Everybody seemed to forget that we had a funeral today...one for Thomas. Fake or not, that shit was scary as fuck.

In true Gallo fashion, they went on as if it were another day.

CHAPTER 30
FREQUENT CUSTOMER CARD

JOE

MY HEAD HAD JUST HIT the pillow when the phone rang. "Joe," Izzy said, out of breath and gasping for air. "Ma's is in the hospital. Hurry." She hung up without telling me anything else.

"Suzy." I shook her, but she didn't respond. "Suzy," I said again, shaking her harder.

"What?" she groaned. "I knew I shouldn't have had that shot of tequila."

I hopped out of bed and grabbed my pants off the floor, trying to put them on. "Ma's in the hospital. I've got to go." My legs were shaking so badly, I could barely keep my balance.

She shot straight up in bed and covered her mouth. "What? Oh my God!" The look of horror on her face probably matched my own when I heard the news. "Is she okay?"

"I have no idea." I yanked a shirt over my head,

not even bothering to see if it was on right. "I'll call as soon as I know anything." I kissed her, leaving her in the bed, and ran out of the house.

By the time I got to the ER waiting room, I looked like roadkill. My hair was standing on end and the shirt I had on was one of Suzy's oversized sleep shirts that said: "I'm Sexy and I Know It."

"What the fuck are you wearing?" Izzy asked as her eyes traveled up and down the length of my body.

I waved my hands. "It doesn't matter. How's Ma?"

"They haven't said anything yet. Daddy's back there with her. Everyone is on their way, but you're the first to make it here."

My hands were shaking and I struggled to breathe. "What happened?" I tried to tame down my locks after a nurse walked back and smirked.

"I don't know. Dad called in tears and said the ambulance was there. He said Ma couldn't breathe."

"Fuck," I whispered and glanced down at the ground. "This can't be happening."

"Joe," Mike said as he ran toward me with Anthony and Thomas, dressed in a hoodie and baseball hat, right on his heels. "What's the word?"

"No news yet."

"I'll get to the bottom of this," he said, pushing me to the side and strutting up to the nurses' station.

I sat down next to Izzy, resting my face in my hands and starting to pray. God and I hadn't been close in years, but with my ma in the hospital, I was willing to grovel.

"They said a doctor will be out to talk with us soon." Mike sat next to me and started to shake his leg and fidget.

Thomas paced the small waiting room area with Anthony. No one spoke, just waited for any tiny shred of hope from the doctors.

My eyes kept going to the clock, checking to see how many minutes had passed since the last time I looked. Minutes turned into an hour, one tick at a time.

Me: No news, sugar.

Suzy: I can't sleep. I'm too worried.
Text me when you hear anything.

Me: I will. Love you.

Thomas stopped in the middle of the floor and pulled at his hair. "What's taking so damn long?"

"Maybe you can sweet-talk that old biddy of a nurse." Mike sneered and pointed toward an old woman sitting behind the reception desk who looked like my grandmother.

"I'll see what I can do." He marched off with his shoulders pushed back. He leaned over the desk and the woman smiled at him, resting her hand under her chin.

Moments later, she stood and walked off to the back. Thomas smiled and blew on his knuckles before rubbing them on his shirt. "Hook, line, and sinker."

"What did you say to her?" I asked, curious how Thomas made headway while Mike didn't.

"Just told her that we'd been waiting an hour and hadn't heard a thing about Ma. She said that someone should've spoken to us by now and she apologized."

Mike's nose wrinkled. "That's it?"

"That's it. I also told her how pretty she looked tonight too."

"Liar," Mike grumbled and crossed his arms over his chest.

"Whatever. It worked, asshat."

"Everyone just shut the fuck up," I said, wiping my hands on my pants and trying to calm down. My heart hadn't stopped racing since the moment the phone rang. "I can't listen to you bicker like little kids right now. Ma could be dying, for all we know."

"Don't you dare say that!" Izzy shot up from her seat and shrieked. "You shut your fucking mouth." Tears pooled in her eyes before breaking free and falling down her cheeks. "I couldn't deal with losing Ma."

"Izzy," I said and held my hand out to her. I pulled her into my lap like I had so many times when she was a scared little girl and comforted her. "She's going to be okay, Izzy. She's a tough woman." I rocked her gently and tried my best to calm her down.

"Gallo?" A nurse standing near the doorway to the patient area said.

We all stood, moving toward her quickly. "Yes?" Izzy was the first to talk.

"Follow me, please." She waved us to follow and we did, not speaking but just moving.

The more steps I took, the harder it became to breathe. Every step took effort as we moved down the corridor. Alarm bells went off, beeping from the heart monitors made my ears hurt, and the staleness of the cold air made each breath a struggle.

The nurse pointed down the hallway. "Room six at the end."

We picked up the pace, unable to wait another moment to find out if the glue that held our family together was alive or dead.

"Mommy," Izzy said, standing near the doorway before disappearing inside.

I inhaled and held the air in my lungs. *Please let her be alive.* When I entered the room, she was sitting upright clutching her left side.

"It's her ribs," Pa said and hung his head, kicking his feet absently. "She broke one and couldn't breathe. I thought she was dying." He rubbed his forehead and grimaced.

"Thank fuck," Mike said and staggered backward, holding his chest.

"Sal, why did you call the kids?" Ma said, trying to adjust, but wincing and grabbing her side.

"Mar, they had a right to know you were in the hospital."

"How the hell did you break a rib, Ma?" Thomas asked, grabbing her hand and holding it in his.

"It was an accident," she said through gritted teeth, her eyes cutting to my father.

"It's my fault." He put his head in his hands. "It's all my fault."

"What did you do, Pop?" I rubbed his back and my heart ached for him. One thing I knew is that he loved her and would never do anything to hurt her.

"I was changing a light bulb and he let go of the ladder," Ma explained, but her eyes shifted.

"Why the fuck were you changing a light bulb this late at night?"

A nurse walked into the room carrying a pair of scrubs for my mother and not paying attention. "Here you go, Mrs. Gallo. This way you don't have to wear that French maid outfit home." When she looked up and noticed us all staring at her with our mouths hanging open, she froze. "Oh, I'm sorry. I didn't mean to—"

"It's okay, dear. Thank you for the clothes."

"What the fuck, you two?" Izzy ran her fingers

through her hair, pulling on it gently. "What really happened?"

"We kind of got a little out of control after a bottle of wine. I went to flip your mom over, she wasn't expecting it, and when I landed on top of her, I may have broken her rib."

I pinched the bridge of my nose and tried to get that visual out of my head. "Jesus!"

"Way to go, Pop." Mike punched him in the shoulder and my father's body rocked back.

"You two really need to find a hobby." Izzy made a gagging sound.

"Or maybe a sex swing," Anthony added.

I walked into the hallway to catch some air and calm my nerves.

> Me: She's fine. Broken rib and will heal.

> Suzy: How did she do that?

> Me: You don't want to know.

> Suzy: I do.

I shook my head, trying to rid myself of the mental picture of them having sex and Ma wearing a French maid getup.

> Me: You don't.

> Suzy: I do.

> Me: Ask Izzy. I'll be home soon.

When I walked back in the room, everyone was kissing them good-bye.

"Want me to stay and help you get her home?" I asked, shoving my phone back in my pocket.

"No, son. I can do it. Go home and get some rest."

"Okay, Pop." I hugged him tightly and turned my attention toward my ma. "No more craziness for you, young lady. Just rest and Suzy will come over tomorrow to help take care of you." Kissing her on the forehead, I thanked God for sparing us from losing her.

"I don't want to put her out." Ma twisted her hands in her lap and frowned. "I can't believe this happened. I guess we're not as young as we used to be, huh, Sal?"

He winked at her and she blushed. "You still got it, though, Mar."

Izzy shook her head and pursed her lips. "And you were giving us shit about our sex lives."

"I don't have little ones at home, Izzy."

"If I remember correctly, that costume is really old." Izzy giggled and covered her mouth.

I pulled her out of the room with me and waved over my shoulder. "Night!" I yelled to them. "Shut up,

Izzy." I smacked her on the back of the head for being a doofus.

CHAPTER 31
SNIP SNIP
SUZY

"JOE, YOU SHOULD BE RESTING." I pushed him back onto the bed and moved the pillow behind his head. "You just had surgery and are on bed rest."

"I had an in-office procedure and I'm fine," he said and sighed, pursing his lips out of frustration.

"The doctor said you needed to take it easy, and I'm going to make sure you do."

"Sugar," he said, pulling me down on top of him. "It was five days ago. The doc said I just needed to avoid strenuous activity for a day or two, not the rest of my life." He swept my hair behind my ear and stared into my eyes. "Wanna make out?" He waggled his eyebrows and smirked.

I smacked his chest and waved my finger in his face. "It's too early."

"It's not," he argued and pushed my hand down.

"It is."

"Doc said usually about a week, but I'm no ordinary man, sugar. My body wants you now. I can't go another day without being inside of you."

I rolled my eyes and tried to get away, but he trapped me. "It's not happening, Joe."

"Suzy," he whispered and put his hands on my face, holding my cheeks in his hands. "I think I deserve a reward for all the pain I went through."

I laughed. "It wasn't that bad."

His thumb caressed the corner of my mouth, and my tongue darted out to taste his skin. "Come on. Since I'm trapped in this bed, I figure we could make use of the time while the babies are asleep." His hips thrust in the air and my eyes followed, noticing he already had a hard-on. "Just like that, but a little lower."

"Do you need me to kiss it and make it better?" I asked, blinking rapidly and playing up the fact that he was in no way in pain.

"Kisses always make everything better." He smirked.

When my eyes glanced over at his length hidden by the sheet, he pulsed his cock, making it almost beckon for me under the sheets. I peeled the sheet back, setting it free, and rubbed my hands together.

The spot was the size of my thumbnail and almost healed. Joe hadn't complained about it for a moment. He wanted to go back to work days ago, but I liked having him with me. I babied him and tried to find ways to keep him at home. I'd use any means necessary, even sex, to have him close for a little while longer.

After I palmed his shaft in my hands, I scurried down the bed to come face-to-face with the reason I fell in love with him in the first place. He made me want him. After a single night in bed with him, I couldn't get him out of my system. It all started with his dick. He knew exactly what he was doing when he took me to bed. Even to this day, he claimed he never meant for me to fall for him, but I called bullshit every time.

My tongue poked out, flicking his piercing, and his hips jerked forward, wanting more. "You have a greedy cock tonight, Mr. Gallo." My cheeks heated and my mouth salivated after just the slightest taste of him.

"My cock is always greedy for you, Mrs. Gallo, but not as greedy as that pussy of yours."

I wiggled my hips, letting my nightie fall forward and exposing my ass to him. "It's lonely," I said, spreading my legs and giving him a glimpse of my wetness.

He smirked and stroked my thighs. "Put your mouth on me." He nudged my lips with his cock and I opened willingly.

Before I had worked my way down his entire length, he stroked my opening and I moaned around his dick, faltering in my movement. I pushed back against his fingers, being the greedy whore that I am, and took him deeper, hoping to be rewarded.

He smacked my ass and I yelped, almost biting down on his cock. I closed my eyes, trying to concentrate as his finger slid into me. I've never been a multitasker, and having his fingers inside of me while trying to blow him threw me off my game.

Using my hand as a guide, I rested my lips against my fingers and pushed myself up and down. My mind started to go hazy, especially when his finger stroked my G-spot.

He grunted, thrusting his cock deeper into my mouth because of my lackluster performance, but he only had himself and his fingers to blame.

I paid special attention to the tip, toying with his piercing with my tongue. He moaned, stroking me deeper and pushing me closer to the edge. I rode his finger, needing just a bit more to get me there, and used the momentum to suck his cock with my lips.

When my body tightened and my orgasm was in reach, I sucked harder, bringing him over the edge with me. We both moaned as our strokes became unsteady with the pleasure.

"Come here," he said as I wiped my lips.

I turned and crawled up his body on shaky legs and arms. "Sorry." My cheeks flushed and I tried to catch my breath.

He grabbed me under the arms and helped me forward. "For what?"

"For doing a bad job."

He laughed softly and pulled my face to his. "Your mouth is perfect. There's no such thing as a bad job when your lips are wrapped around me, sugar."

I smiled and stared into his eyes. "I love you, Joe."

"I love you too." He kissed my lips before adjusting our bodies.

I settled into the crook of his arm and felt at peace for the first time in months. The turmoil seemed to follow us, seeping into our lives when we least expected it.

"Do you think we'll be like your parents when we're old?" My fingers touched his piercing, turning it gently.

His hand wrapped tighter around my shoulder. "You mean wearing French maid outfits and breaking ribs?"

"Yeah." I giggled at the thought.

"I hope so."

"Me too."

His hand stopped moving against my skin. "Sugar?"

I curled tighter against him. "Yeah, Joe?"

"Can we not talk about what happened to my parents again?"

"Sure. We'll never talk about it again."

"Thank fuck," he growled. "It's an image I'm afraid I'll never wipe from my mind."

I wanted to grow old with him, surrounded by our children and their children and driving them insane with stories like this one.

Ten years ago, I never would've dreamed that this would be my life. I felt like an outsider in my own family growing up, but being with the Gallos made me feel like I belonged to something bigger and better.

I had everything I'd ever dreamed of and more.

I'd finally found my home.

Izzy & James are back for one more journey? The saga continues in **WORSHIP ME.**

Visit **menofinked.com/worship-me** *to learn more.*

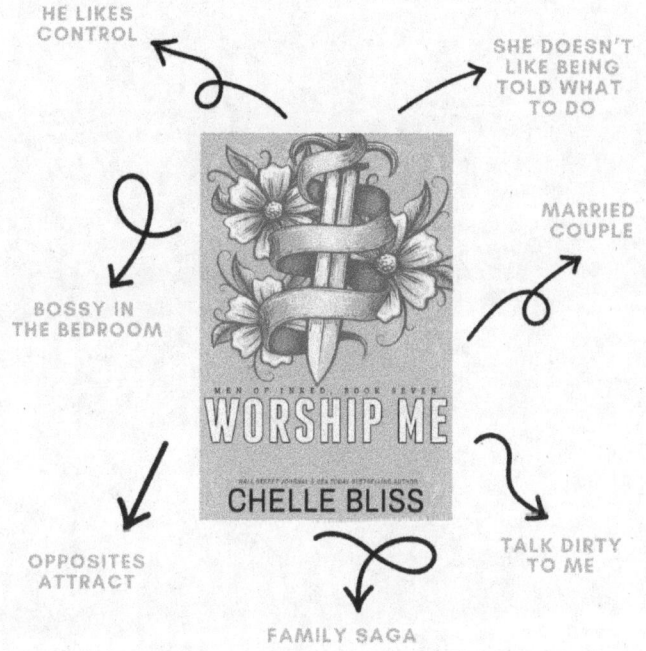

HE LIKES
CONTROL

SHE DOESN'T
LIKE BEING
TOLD WHAT
TO DO

MARRIED
COUPLE

BOSSY IN
THE BEDROOM

OPPOSITES
ATTRACT

TALK DIRTY
TO ME

FAMILY SAGA

I hope you loved City, Suzy, and the Gallo Family. The family's story continues in **WORSHIP ME!**

When a case takes a dangerous turn, James is forced to get Izzy involved in an undercover sting that will test her sexual boundaries along with their relationship.

Izzy & James are back for one more journey? The saga continues in **WORSHIP ME.**

Visit ***menofinked.com/worship-me*** *to learn more.*

BECOME A MEMBER OF THE FAMILY...

Want a place to talk romance books, meet other bookworms, and all things Men of Inked? Join Chelle Bliss Books on Facebook to get sneak peeks, exclusive news, and special giveaways.

Want to be the first to hear about the next Men of Inked book or everything Chelle Bliss? Join my newsletter by visiting _menofinked.com/ inked-news_ or scan the QR code below.

ABOUT THE AUTHOR

I'm a full-time writer, time-waster extraordinaire, social media addict, coffee fiend, and ex-history teacher. *To learn more about my books, please visit menofinked.com.*

Want to stay up-to-date on the newest
Men of Inked release and more?
Join my newsletter at *menofinked.com/news*

Join over 10,000 readers on Facebook in Chelle Bliss Books private reader group and talk books and all things reading. Come be part of the family!

See the Gallo Family Tree

Where to Follow Me:

- facebook.com/authorchellebliss1
- instagram.com/authorchellebliss
- bookbub.com/authors/chelle-bliss
- goodreads.com/chellebliss
- tiktok.com/@chelleblissauthor
- amazon.com/author/chellebliss

♥ Men of Inked Reader Guide ♥

Visit **_menofinked.com/guide_** to download the Men of
Inked Reading guide, featuring a printable reading guide, the
family tree, and information about each Gallo family saga read.